WHATEVER HAPPENED TO JAVI HORATA?

DAVID B. LYONS

ISBN: 978-1-7384519-1-3

Created with Vellum

JAVI

I did not want to take them. That is the truth. The real truth. If I had the choice to be a normal man with a normal job and a normal family and a normal life, then I would not have taken them. Honest to God above, I would not have taken them.

I am not a bad man. I used to not be a bad man. Before today. But I just... it was just so easy. Like taking candy from a baby. Or giving candy to a baby. Which is what I did.

I look over my shoulder. Into the back seat of the car and I stare at the satchel again. Then I stare above it, out the back window. To make sure that man in the ugly yellow jacket isn't following me. He jumped into the river. Thinking he could catch up with a speedboat. I saw him trying to get out two minutes later. Gripping onto the grass. That's when I thought I better run for it. I better get to the car. Get out of here as soon as I could.

Honest to God above, I am not a bad man. I am not. I just needed that satchel. It's the other people who are the bad people. The people who run corporations. The people who run big businesses. The people who run politics. They are the ones who make sure the little people like me can't get jobs. Can't afford houses. Can't afford dinners.

That's why I had those mints on me this morning. I found them when I was looking through the bins for some food. For some fruit. I usually find half-eaten apples in the bin. Sometimes some unfinished fast food still in the container. That's my favourite find. Because fast food stays warm when it is in a container.

I just need to think about that satchel. That way I will forget about those two children. I will forget their little faces. The dry tears on their cheeks.

She was happy and smiley at first. She was actually happy that I was talking to her. That I offered her a mint. Then when I suggested she come to my car for more candy, she came with me... She walked right behind me all the way to the car. That's how easy it was. I didn't mean to take a kid today. I was just walking towards the orphanage. To see how easy it might be. To see if I could do it. To see if I could really carry it out if it ever came to that. It was easy to buy the rope and the black duct tape. Anybody can do that. I had it in my car for two weeks before today. I bought it in Gnacko's Hardware. For just eight euros. Thinking one day I might try it. One day I might try to snatch a kid. Just so I could start a proper life.

I would not have known about snatching kids if I had never been in prison. In prison you learn all sorts of new tricks. How silly is it to gather all of the criminals together, and put them in the same building for twenty-four hours a day? How idiotic are the people who run prisons? Who run politics? How fucking idiotic can they be? I would never have thought of snatching a kid if it wasn't for the ugly men I met behind bars. It was sitting on the benches at the canteen in C-Wing of Pankrac prison where I learned about the market.

That's where I first heard that you could make ten times more money from snatching a kid than you could by holding up a bank. Or a post office. And it's easier. Much easier. And less risky. There are cameras all over banks and post offices. That's how I got caught the last time. But in the fields, in the rural suburbs, there are no cameras. There are no risks. Not really. I didn't think there were any risks at all until the siren came towards those speedboats.

It's as simple as stealing candy from a baby. Or giving candy to a baby. Which is what I did. And now I have fifty thousand euro filling the satchel in the backseat of the car I stole.

I am literally on my way to starting a new life. I'm going back to Portugal. Back to where it all began. Before I ran away. Before I ran away from my father's fists. And his belts. I can still feel his belts whipping my back anytime I think back that far. I can feel that pain anytime I want...

I stare into the rear-view mirror to see that the narrow road behind me is still empty. That idiot in the yellow jacket is nowhere near me. I'll be out of these country fields in twenty minutes. Then out of Prague twenty minutes after that. Then across the border one more hour after that. Then I'll be free... free to start the life I should have started many years ago, years before I started getting into trouble.

It is just a shame I had to steal two children to start this life. I didn't want to take them... I didn't. I was just walking. Honest to God above, I was just walking through the fields towards the orphanage. To see if it was easy to snatch a kid. To see if kids might fracture and split up. To see if it was possible to find one walking alone. Then I did see one walking alone. About a mile before I reached the orphanage. Walking straight towards me. A little blonde. Tiny, tiny little girl.

'Would you like a mint?' I asked her.

She didn't pause.

She stuck out her hand. And I pulled the mints out of my pocket and popped one from the top for her to take. Her face went all funny as she sucked on it.

'It's nice,' she said.

I looked around the fields. It was just the two of us. Just me and the tiny, little blonde girl. And all I saw in her face was fifty-thousand euro.

'You hungry?' I asked.

'I'm really hungry,' she said.

'Okay,' I said. My heart was thumping. 'Follow me.'

LENNY

16:25

Lenny's pupils have dilated, and his eyeballs are bulging wide as he stares intently at the tarmac road stretching and winding ahead.

'Holy fucking shit,' he pants to himself, his breathing sharp and heavy.

He darts his pupils to the rear-view mirror, to see the river distancing in the horizon behind before he glances down at the digital speedometer between his steering wheel, watching the sixties turn into the seventies.

'Holy fucking shit,' he shouts when the car begins to shake and crunch beneath him. He yanks the steering-wheel left, sharply, then right sharply, his head darting side-to-side as tall wisps of yellow grass begin to flick at the car's windows.

'Holy fucking shit!' he calls out again, stamping on the brake, spinning the BMW to a skidding halt.

The dilated pupils dart around his bulging eyes before he glares over his shoulder to the road he thought he was driving on.

The road he would be driving on had the speedometer not stolen his attention.

He spins in his seat, his wet puffer jacket squeaking, to stare toward the river now lost in the distance, wondering which child it is Olette is hugging on the cold deck of a small speedboat back there. He wants to know, *desperately* wants to know...

He pauses, sucks a deep inhale to his lungs, before whistling it through his chapped lips. Then he spins back around, grips the steering wheel tight and steps firmly on the gas pedal, the back wheels of the brand-spanking new BMW sliding and skidding against the murky earth until they speed forward.

When the car clunks its way back onto the flat road it begins to purr; the seventies on the speedometer turning into the eighties as Lenny continues his pursuit of Javi Horata.

The investigator wiggles his soaked backside in the driver's seat before shaking his shoulders, attempting to loosen the white shirt gluing to his skin. He feels terrible. Wet. Cold. Humiliated. The pain of missing one of the speedboats casting a dark shadow over the incredible work he carried out to prevent the other child from being trafficked. He pulls at the collar of his white shirt again as the car speeds then stabs a finger at the dashboard, turning on the air conditioning. When lukewarm air blows from the vents, hitting his hands either side of the steering wheel, Lenny removes one of them to pop open a pocket on his heavy yellow jacket, pulling out his phone screen. Then he shovels the same hand into the opposite pocket to retrieve the battery.

Conscious of his off-road experience minutes prior, he keeps his stare on the winding tarmac ahead while he clicks the battery back into place with just one hand, then he holds down the button on the side of the phone, turning the power back on. *Hopefully* turning the power back on. A cringe runs down his damp spine as the slap his jacket made when it flopped against the choppy river water plays in his ears.

'Uuuugh,' he says, wiggling his body again.

The Apple logo blinks onto his screen, gifting Lenny some hope. But the logo isn't blinking the phone back to life. It's stuck.... Jammed. Not moving beyond the white apple.

'Fuck,' he hisses, tossing the phone to the passenger seat.

When he glances at the speedometer, the eighties are turning into the nineties, and he recalls the black BMW — similar to the one he was driving right now - screeching to a stop outside Javi Horata's house a little over an hour ago. It's only been five hours since Lenny started this job. With one page of notes to go on. Now he's in a high-speed chase on a narrow rural road in one of those BMWs, chasing a child trafficker in a maze of the most southern regions of Prague.

Suddenly, out of the corner of his eye, he sees it. His phone blinking back to life. His apps appearing on the screen in front of a black and white portrait of his twin boys' wide grins.

He snatches the phone from the passenger seat again and stabs his thumb to an app, *any* app, just to test the response.

'Yes! Fuck yes!' he calls out, bringing the screen to his lips and kissing it. 'You waterproof mother fucker.'

He glances back up at the road ahead, composes himself with an elongated inhale, then clicks into the Amazon group chat to see if there has been any update from the children... any child... whichever child it is that was on the speedboat that got away.

But there's nothing.

He tuts, before stabbing his finger at the call log button, then touching the same finger against a phone number at the top of the page.

'Hello, People Trafficking Unit,' a strange voice says.

'My name is Private Investigator Lenny Moon,' he says. 'I started as a PI with the PTU this morning. I have been working with Olette. May I ask you to please put me through to her mobile number straight away?'

'Olette Lee?'

'Yes.'

There's a silence. Before a fidgeting noise finally leads to a ringing tone.

'Hello,' a familiar voice says, answering.

'Olette.'

'Lenny,' she says, 'Lenny is that you?'

'Olette,' he says, his breathing growing heavy again, the grip of his other hand tightening around the steering wheel, his knuckles pale. 'Olette, which child did you save?'

JAVI

Honest to God above, I hated to do it. To push her into the back of the car. To put tape across her mouth. To tie her hands to that bed. Honest to God above, I hated to do it. My heart was thumping all the way through. But it was thumping most of all downstairs when I was walking back and forward in my old living-room, squeezing the phone in my hand. Angry with myself. But excited for myself. Wondering if I should do it. Wondering if I could do it. If I could make that call. I could have let her go. Or I could have dialled that number. I did not know what to do. Honest to God above. I didn't. I walked and walked and walked up and down and up and down my empty living-room. Up and down. Up and down. Squeezing that phone in my hand, asking myself the same two questions over and over, again and again. Was that a little girl lying in the bed upstairs? Or fifty-thousand euro? Enough money for me to start a new life.

'Vot is your calling for?' he said as soon as he answered. My hands were sweating. And I was still gripping the phone really tight. Pressing it to my ear now. I didn't know if I was going to say what I did say next. Not until I said it.

'I have cargo—'

'Von moment.'

The line clicked, and then it went quiet. Maybe for ten seconds. Maybe thirty. I could have hung up while it was quiet. I thought about hanging up. I probably kept thinking about hanging up until the line clicked again.

'Cargo?'

'Uh-huh,' I said. 'A girl.'

'How old?' he said.

I took the phone from my ear and looked up to the ceiling, towards the bedroom above me.

'Seven,' I guessed.

'Von moment.'

There was a click on the line again. But by this time I was calm. I wasn't sweating. And I wasn't pacing up and down and up and down. Not anymore. I wasn't going to hang up now. I had already told them I had a girl. About seven years of age.

'Ve vill contact you on the number you rang from vith further information.'

'No... Wait!' I said. 'How much would uh—'

'Ve vill talk about money vhen ve next contact you.'

'Oh, okay. I was informed there was a fixed amount. I was told there was a fixed amount if I snatched a kid.'

'Nuh.'

That's all he said. He grunted it down the line. His accent was thick. Really thick. And difficult to place. Perhaps Dutch. Perhaps German. Or Austrian. I didn't care. I only cared that I was going to get the fifty-thousand euro I was told I would get if I snatched a child.

He rang back maybe five minutes later.

'Von moment,' he said as soon as I answered.

After a click, another voice appeared on the line. A different one. No longer speaking English in a thick Dutch or German accent. But speaking Czech. The language I've learned well since moving here.

He told me the offer for my girl was thirty-thousand euro. Not the fifty I had been told it would be when I was in prison. He told me the days of fifty-thousand-euro fees for snatched kids were pre-pandemic. An offer that belongs in the past. Long before COVID.

'But I need fifty-thousand to start my new life,' I told him.

He did not care. I would only get thirty-thousand. Unless... unless I snatched another child. A boy. Boy and girl combinations can reach up to eighty-thousand, he told me. That sure would start my new life.

I had already done it once. So, I thought doing it again may not be as scary as it was the first time. But it was. It was even scarier. I drove round and round for a long, long time trying to find a boy. Until I saw him.... lost on the streets of the inner-city, in his little Manchester United football jersey.

'You lost, boy?' I asked him, winding my window down.

'Is uh... is The Grand Hotel this way?' he asked.

I didn't want to do it. Honest to God above I didn't want to do it. But I did. I leaned across my car and opened the passenger door.

'It's uh, it's not that far... let me drive you,' I said. I said it nice. As nice as I could in my best English.

He looked around while my heart thumped and thumped. Then he got in the passenger seat and closed the door and smiled up at me.

I did not want to take him. Honest to God above, I did not want to. I had to. If I didn't take him and her, the two of them, I'd still have to live my shitty life in Prague with no money, no job, no food, no nothing. This is my only chance. My only chance of getting a life. A new life. Any life...

I look back over my shoulder at the satchel in the back seat again, then up to the back windscreen. Still nobody is behind me. Nobody is near me. Maybe nobody is chasing me through these old fields. Maybe I will make it all the way to Portugal without being chased.

I didn't hate Portugal when I used to live there. I only hated my house. My home. My sad mother. My drunk father. I don't know why they hated me so much. I should have run away long, long before I did. But now that they are both dead, I can go back. I can go back home. Back to Portugal. Back where it all began, to start a new life with that satchel lying on the back seat.

I was eighteen when I ran away. I should have run away when I was fifteen. I would have saved myself a lot of broken noses. And broken memories. I moved to Spain at first. I took a train direct to Madrid from Lisbon and spent two years lying in a sleeping bag on the corner of Mayor Street, outside the McDonalds, hoping some nice people out of the many thousands who walked by would drop some coins into my hat. Sometimes I would get enough money to buy three meals a day. Sometimes I wouldn't get enough to buy one. It was the same when I moved to France. I went down south, to Nice—where all the rich people live. I learned rich people are rich because they don't give any of their money away. I stayed on the beach in Nice for three months eating leftover food from the bins before I snuck on a train I had no idea was going to leave me in Prague. A city I have lived in for the past twenty-five years. At first on the streets, before I got a job in a kitchen. It was one of the chefs in that kitchen who helped me apply for housing—and two and a half years later, I finally got a key. A key to 78 Zdarska Street. The home I left this morning for the very last time. I couldn't keep living there. They want me gone. The government. Because my work credits ran out. I tried to find work. To keep up with the payments. I tried everywhere. That is how I know the system sets up poor people to fail. How are we supposed to get experience for work, if we can't get work in the first place? That's why I ended up stealing from post offices. Stealing from shops. I had no choice. But if you steal shops and post offices, you end up in prison. And prison is where I learned that stealing from shops and post offices was a stupid thing to do.

'Snatch a child,' Old Bryny said to me one day in the prison canteen.

Old Bryny was probably a bit of a pervert. I am not. I do not want to do anything with the children. I hear that most of the people who traffic kids don't want to do anything to them. They just want money. I think. I hope. I just want money anyway. That's why I did what I did, God. I did it for the satchel in the back seat. I did it to make my life better.

I try not to think about it too much. About them. About their two little faces. So, I shake my head before I turn around to stare at the bulges in the satchel again, when something catches my eye—a flicker that makes me squint through the rear windscreen. A flicker in the distance. A flicker that turns into a car. A black car. A black BMW.

LIAM

He grips the back of my jersey and drags me forward, pushing me and hurting me. Hurting my back. Just below my neck. But I feel excited. Not scared. Because the siren is coming. Lenny Moon is coming. To save us. Finally.

I look over my shoulder as I'm being dragged and see that Sofie is being dragged, too. To the other boat. Just like I thought. As soon as I saw the two boats, I knew we were going to be separated.

'Sofie!' I call out. But she can't hear me. Not over the siren.

I am pushed hard over the side of the boat, and my face lands on the hard rubber. It's sore. But I don't mind the pain. I get back to my feet and spin around, seeing the black car stopping. Then the siren stops. And a man in a yellow coat gets out and begins to run towards me. Running to save me. The man who pushed me onto the boat climbs over the rim and then goes to the front, pulling a black lever. Trying to start the engine. Trying to get away. I run towards him low, like they do in rugby, and I tackle him, pushing him with my shoulder. Really hard. So hard he trips over the edge of the boat and splashes into the river. I jump up and down excited. Excited because I'm going to be saved. Me and Sophie. We're going to be saved. That's when I hear it. While I'm jumping up and down on the spot excited. The other boat's engine. Starting. And then it pulls off, spraying water back at me, taking Sofie away.

I watch as the man in the yellow jacket dives in. As if he thinks he can catch up with a speedboat.

'No!' I fall to my knees. 'Sofffieeee!'

I cry. Because she will be so scared. So scared without me.

I wipe my eyes with the shoulders of my jersey and when I am trying to suck the tears back up my nose, I hear her. Breathing heavily. Running. Then jumping. Over the rim and onto the boat.

'Liam?' she says.

I stare up at her as she steps towards me. She has a face like my Auntie Sue. Nice eyes. Kind eyes. She hugs me, wrapping her arms around my back, rubbing me to keep warm.

'You're safe now,' she whispers.

She rubs my back while I cry into her shoulder. And my breathing shakes like my body is shaking.

'She has the Kindle,' I say, sobbing. 'Sofie still has the Kindle. I made sure she took it. She'll be okay. Won't she?'

The woman doesn't say anything. She just hugs me tighter, rubbing her hand in circles on my back. Trying to stop me from shaking so much.

'Will you find her?' I ask, crying. 'Will you find Sofie?'

I lean back to look into her kind eyes.

'We will,' she says, nodding.

And then I nod.

'My name is Olette,' she says. 'I'm an investigator with the People Trafficking Unit. We investigate missing people.'

'Like Lenny Moon?' I ask.

She nods and then looks over the side of the boat, her arms still wrapped around me. And I know. I know Lenny Moon is the man in the yellow coat. The man who dived into the river, trying to save Sofie.

When I stand back up, I look over the rim too. To see Lenny Moon's bald head bobbling on the water. And when I squint further ahead, I can only see it as a dot. Sofie's speedboat. Miles away. Miles and miles away already.

'Please tell me you'll find her,' I say, my voice shaking.

'We will,' Olette says. Then she squeezes me again, and I rest my head against her coat.

Lenny Moon shouts something up to us. But I can't understand what he's saying. Not with the wind. And when I look up at Olette, I see that she hasn't heard him either. Because she has her phone to her ear.

'Hello,' she says, looking down at me. Her eyes are so like my Auntie Sue's. The same shape. Same colour. 'One moment.' She smiles her kind eyes at me. 'It's for you,' she says. Then she holds the phone to my ear.

'Hello,' I say.

'Liam,' he says. 'Liam? Is that you?'

'Da?' I say, sobbing.

'Liam. Where are ye? Where the hell did you get to?'

'I'm fine,' I say, crying. Sobbing. Tears pouring down my face. 'A policewoman found me. I'm safe. I'm safe, Da.'

I hear him crying. Which is really weird. Because Da never cries. Ever. He didn't even cry when his da died.

'I'm so...' I hear him breathing hard, trying to not cry. 'I'm so... Jesus, we've been up the walls, Liam. We thought, we thought... I don't know what we thought. When can I... when can I hug you?'

'Hug me,' I say? And then I stop crying. To laugh. Da never hugs me. He's definitely never asked when can he hug me.

'Soon,' Olette says, staring her kind eyes down at me. 'We'll get you back to The Grand Hotel as soon as we can.'

'Soon,' I say, spraying tears into Olette's phone. 'I'll be back in the hotel soon.'

'Oh Jesus, Liam,' Da says.

'Da?' I say.

'Yeah?' he says, sniffing.

'Are we still going to the zoo today?'

LENNY

16:43

Lenny grips the steering wheel tight with one hand while the other presses the phone tight against his ear.

'Liam feels more upset for Sofie than he feels relieved for himself,' Olette says. 'He's an impressive child. Mature for his age.'

'I'm so glad you found him,' Lenny whispers into his phone.

'Well, it was you who found him,' she says. 'It was you who led this investigation.'

'I've gotta find out where that second speedboat is going!' Lenny says, exasperated.

He was sick of saying that exact sentence. It was the fifth time he had said that exact sentence on this phone call alone.

'You will,' she tells him. 'First you got to catch that bastard.'

Lenny could hear the shake in Olette's voice, not just from the cold of the riverbank, but from the enormity of the task at hand. Her voice had been quivering since she answered Lenny's call five minutes ago. She had told him that Liam's only concern from the moment she had first hugged him on the speedboat was the welfare of Sofie Le Saux. The girl he had spent three hours tied up with. On a bed. And then in the back of a car. Olette had posed questions to the boy before Lenny had rung, hoping for clues that may lead them to Sofie. But Liam knew little. Relatively little. He could describe the men. Briefly. Horata — as they already knew — had a scruffy brown beard. One of the drivers of the speedboats had long, thick black hair down to his shoulders. The other had a red woollen hat on. Lenny knew it was the one in the hat who ended up overboard when he and Olette arrived at the scene. Because he saw the hat bobbling in the river. That informed Lenny that Sofie Le Saux was currently heading to who-knows-where on a speedboat being driven by a man who had long, thick black hair down to his shoulders. Not much to go on. Which is why it's vital that the black BMW Lenny was currently driving caught up with the blue box-saloon it was chasing.

'An ambulance and two more cars from the PTU are on the way here,' Olette says. 'Maybe ten more minutes out. Soon as you give me any update on where you are, I'll get a car to join you, Lenny... make sure we catch this bastard.'

'I'm gonna catch him, Olette,' Lenny says sternly, his focus on the narrow road winding ahead. 'I promise you. I promise Liam. And I promise Sofie. I'm gonna catch Horata. Then I'm going to find her. You tell Liam that. Tell him I won't stop until I find Sofie Le Saux.'

He pinches a thumb against the red button, then tosses the phone to the passenger seat before washing a hand over his stubbly face. His eyes squint the length of the narrow road ahead as he imagines the innocent face of the pretty girl on the one-sheet Chuck Volgt handed him in the lobby of the PTU this morning. There wasn't much to go on then, and yet Lenny still made huge strides in this investigation. And here he was, some six hours later, having rescued one child, and in hot pursuit of the man who knows where the other one is being taken to. Fine investigating. Even if it discomforts Lenny to swallow such a conscious compliment.

He wiggles in the seat again to rid his mind of the discomfort, his damp clothes still weighing heavy, still gluing to his skin. It's when he is shuffling his shoulders, shivering, that he begins to squint even more. Focusing ahead. At a dot. A dot turning into a blue box. A blue boxed-car.

'Got you, you mother fucker,' Lenny says to himself.

He grips the steering wheel tight with both hands, stepping even firmer on the gas. And as the electric engine whirrs, Lenny notices that Horata has clocked him in his rear-view mirror and is now desperately trying to push the blue car to its limits. But he stands no chance. Not up against the modern BMW hovering and purring above the narrow tarmac.

As the blue car gets bigger, Lenny pushes both palms to the car horn.

'Pull over. You are under arrest. Pull over!' he shouts.

He fidgets at the door, to wind down his window, then sticks his bald head out.

'Pull over!' he screams.

When he realises he can't even hear himself, he winds the window back up, then yanks the steering wheel to the left, pressing firmer on the gas, causing the engine strain. And when his BMW aligns with Horata's blue car, he tries shouting again.

'Pull over! Pull over!'

Horata doesn't even look his way, his gaze forward, hopelessly willing his boxy saloon car to quicken.

Then, in the huff of an exhausted exhale, Lenny realises he has no choice. He yanks the steering wheel right... to a crunch, a thud, and then a screech as both cars skid to a crashing halt, the side of the blue-box car heavily dented, steam rising from its bonnet as an Air Bag punches at Lenny's face.

SOFIE

I feel scared and excited when he runs towards me. So, so scared. And so, so excited. At the same time. I watch as he runs past the boat Liam is in, shouting back at the woman running behind him and I know he is running to come save me first. To be my hero. And my friend.

A horrible noise frightens me. And I know. I know it's my boat. My boat shaking. My boat about to take off before private investigator Lenny Moon can save me.

'Nooo!' I scream, turning to the man with the long hair. 'Noooooo!'

I look back around as the boat speeds off and see private investigator Lenny Moon diving into the river. I try to walk towards the back of the speedboat, the Kindle still gripped between my fingers behind my back, falling and stumbling, hoping to see him swimming fast after me. Coming to save me. But when I look up he isn't swimming. He didn't even start swimming. His bald head is just bobbing above the white water we've left behind. Far behind.

As we speed off faster, I fall back again. Flat on to my back.

And the Kindle slaps behind me and slides to the other side of the speedboat.

'Noooo!' I scream. 'Noooo!'

I turn my face in the rubber floor of the boat and cry into it as the boat speeds up the river, rocking. Now I'm all alone. No Liam next to me. No private investigator Lenny Moon chasing after me. Or swimming after me. He's just bobbing up and down on the river. Probably as lost as I am. I think it was private investigator Lenny Moon anyway. He was the one who ran fastest out of the black police car. And it was private investigator Lenny Moon who told me he was coming to save me. So it must be him. It must be him bobbing up and down on the river. Far away from me. Far, far away from me.

I turn my face and look at the Kindle on the opposite side of the speedboat. And my shoulders shake. Because of the fright. And because of the rocking. Then, I start rolling towards it, my hands behind my back, my body tumbling over and over and over.

When I reach the Kindle, I try to pinch it between my fingers, but it's not easy. Not with all of this rocking. So I just sit my backside on top of it, and I cry. And cry. So many tears. So, so many tears for so many different things.

As the boat speeds along, spraying water up and over at me like it's raining, I think about what would happen if I just jumped in. If I just jumped over the side rim of this speedboat, into the white water. What would happen? I would probably just sink. Sink to the bottom and drown and die. I've only ever swam in a paddling pool. A paddling pool they used to blow up in the garden of the Paris orphanage in the summer. On hot days. Hot days only. I swam one side to the other of the paddling one time. Without any help. But I don't think I could swim in this river. Not from one side to the other. Even if my hands weren't tied behind my back.

I huff, then I look back at him. The long-haired man at the

front of the boat, his hair blowing behind him. And I wonder where he's taking me. That wherever it is will have to be a better place than jumping into the river and sinking to the bottom. So I suck up my tears, and I wipe my eyes as much as I can with my shoulders.

'It's okay, Sofie,' I say to myself as I turn over and begin to lie flat over the Kindle, feeling it against my tummy. This will save me. I can still text private investigator Lenny Moon. Later. Whenever it is I can get my hands untied. I'll text him more clues. More clues about where it is I have been taken to. Then he'll come and save me. And be my friend.

JAVI

My face flies forward. Almost touching the steering wheel. Then my body snaps back to the seat. Fast. Fast and hard. And everything goes silent. Silent and still. As if there hasn't just been a big car crash. A car smash. I look around myself, then down my body to make sure I feel good. Then my eyes look at the rear-view mirror and I see his little bald head poking out of the top of his ugly yellow jacket in the car behind. Holding his face... both hands over his face...

I shake my head, then I turn the key in the ignition. But the car roars. A horrible noise. And it doesn't move. It can't move.

'Fuck!' I roar.

I turn the key. To try it again.

'Prosim, prosim, prosim...' I whisper. 'Please.'

The engine roars. A horrible roar again. Then there's a loud scrape as the car tries to go forward, then collapses on one side.

I take the key out quickly, then turn around to grab the satchel before opening the door and stepping out. I can see all the damage along the side, half of my car caved in, the back wheel collapsed. When I look up at him, he still has his both hands over his face. I wonder why he is not moving. Why he's not coming for me. But I don't wait around to find out. I turn, and I run. I run as fast as I can across the yellow field hooking my arms into the straps of the satchel. When I look over my shoulder, I expect him to be chasing me. But he still hasn't got out of his car.

I wonder if he knows who I am. If he knows my name. And which child they rescued. That idiot with the ugly yellow jacket now holding his face in the car behind me tried to dive into the river after one of the speedboats. But it was away from him even before his ugly yellow jacket got wet. The other speedboat was still at the riverbank. It hadn't taken off before I decided to get out of hiding. If they did save one of the children, then he'll probably know who I am by now. The police are probably already inside 78 Zdarska Street. Raiding the empty home I left behind. They won't find much. They won't find anything. A battered sofa. An old TV. That's all that's left of my old life. The life I had before I snatched two children.

'Honest to God,' I say, staring up towards the grey sky as I run, 'I did not mean to take them.'

I had to. I had to take them. I had no choice. I had to get enough money to buy myself a new life. The fifty-thousand euro on my back will give me that new life. I should have got more money. I told the man when I arrived at Vlatva and Labe that I had been promised eighty thousand for a boy and a girl combo. He said I was talking shit. That nobody gets eighty thousand for two children anymore. They wanted to give me forty thousand. I shouted in the man's face. And told him I will take the two children back to Prague. Let them out in the city centre to find their own way home. Wherever home is. An orphanage for the little blonde girl. Cork in Ireland for the chatty, annoying boy.

He eventually agreed to pay fifty-thousand, so I shook his hand and thought I would get out of Vlatva as quickly as I could. But as I was about to leave, the black police car came, its sirens flashing. I hid in the bushes along the riverbank, and when I saw the idiot in the yellow jacket diving into the river, I thought that was my chance. So, I ran. I ran for my car and sped away as fast as I could. Until he caught up with me. Crashed into me.

I turn around again. And see that he is out of the car. Running towards me.

'Fuck,' I say, sprinting faster, towards the forest ahead of me.

If I get into the forest, I can lose him. I can run in any direction. Left, right. Forward. Even backward. Around trees. Thousands of trees. He won't be able to see any of my moves. I'll shake him off. Get out of here. Get my new life started.

'Horata!' I hear him shout. 'You're under arrest!'

They do know who I am! Shit! They work fast. I was going to change my identity anyway. Now I know I have to. I'll shave my beard. Cut my hair. Maybe I shouldn't restart my life in Portugal now. If they know who I am, they'll know where I'm from. Portugal might be the first place they look for me.

'Fuck,' I shout, as I reach the first tree, gripping it so I can spin around to see him. He's maybe two hundred metres behind. His arms moving fast by his side as he runs.

I push the tree away and disappear, running from tree to tree, going in different directions, making sure that when he gets into the forest he will have no idea where I am.

It's grey in here. And misty. Easy to get lost in.

'Horata,' I hear him shout. My name echoes through the forest. And I stop. In shock. And hide behind a tree.

LENNY

17:11

Lenny cups a hand either side of his mouth.

'Horata!' he shouts.

His booming voice reverberates around the tall Corsican pine trees, until there's a still and a silence again.

He shuffles forward, his head still dizzy from the crash, his mind still wandering in a maze of directions. A maze of directions is literally what he could take right now. Around any of the thousands of trees blocking his path though the grey, misty forest.

'Horata!' Lenny shouts again. He listens until the echo fades to a silence again, then he swings around a tree and decides to walk in the direction it leaves him facing.

As he jogs, Lenny rubs his face, still trying to awaken from the punch of the Air Bag. He's not sure how long he was out cold, sitting upright in the BMW, his hands over his face, but he came around in time to see Horata racing for the forest Lenny now finds himself lost in.

He stops behind one of the tall trunks to listen intently, in hope of hearing the snapping of any twigs under any foot. Or maybe a heavy breath grunting for air. But the distant cawking of the German crows circling the grey sky somewhere above the mist, is all he can hear.

So, instead of calling out 'Horata' as loudly as he can again, Lenny takes his mobile phone from his heavy, damp yellow jacket pocket, and stabs at the screen before lifting it to his ear.

'Hello, People Trafficking Unit.'

'It's me.... Again,' he whispers. 'Lenny Moon. I'm a new private investigator. You put me through to Olette Lee's mobile phone earlier. Can you do the same again?'

'One moment, PI Moon,' the voice says.

Lenny waits in the eerie, silent forest, the phone pressed to his ear, staring up the length of the pine trees before they vanish into the greyness.

'I'm sorry PI Moon, Miss Lee is not answering right now, let me send her mobile number to the phone you are ringing from, will that suffice?'

'Indeed,' Lenny says. 'Please.'

He hangs up and palms the phone before darting his eyes around the trees. When the phone vibrates in his hand, he stares at the screen, hits SAVE to the contact details he's just received and then types in her name: OLETTE LEE.

He shuffles himself forward, then darts his eyes around a different angle of the trees, the ringing tone trilling in his ear until it cuts. Olette's not answering.

He swipes out of his call log with a tut, then stabs his way back to the Amazon Customer Services Chat, disappointed to see there hasn't been a message sent for over an hour now. The Kindle may no longer be in play. Which means Lenny's only chance of rescuing Sofie comes down to him finding Horata somewhere amongst this maze of lanky tree trunks.

When he pockets his phone, he closes his eyes, imagining the pretty face of the little girl on the one-sheet he was handed this morning. That pretty face was, right this very minute, being whisked somewhere, anywhere, on a speedboat. Scared for her life. From where Vlatva meets Labe, Sofie Le Saux could be travelling in any one of dozens of directions through Europe while Lenny was stood hopelessly squinting around grey trees.

He shakes his head, ridding his mind of the pretty face by flipping over the one sheet. An orphan from the Milkova Orphanage.

'Mother fucker,' Lenny whispers to himself.

He knows Horata would have preyed on an orphan purposely. So that there'd be no family willing to do whatever it took for as long as it took to track down the bastard who swiped their child. Yet it doesn't make sense that he would later swipe a boy from a holidaying family. It seemed to Lenny that Horata was likely operating on a whim this morning. And is still operating on a whim right now. Somewhere inside this forest. Guessing his way out of here.

'I gotta find this mother fucker,' Lenny whispers.

Then he shuffles forward, stopping every few strides to listen. Suddenly he hears a crunch. A crunch. Crunch. Crunch. Somebody running. Ahead of him. So, he sprints, chicaning through the trees, racing, and pacing in the direction of the noise.

'Horata!' he shouts, huffing and puffing, his hands whizzing either side of the heavy yellow jacket. He sprints. And sprints. Until... from behind the trunk of a tall tree, a fist swings towards his face. Catching him on the chin. And his back slaps to the forest bed.

JAVI

The pain is getting worse and worse. Up and down my arm. But I have to forget about it and keep running. And running. As fast as I can. As far as can. Away from where I left his body lying in the forest.

I caught him with the inside of my wrist. Hard. And he fell back. Straight back. As if he was dead. I don't know how to punch. I've never punched anybody. Not since school. But he just came running towards me, really, really fast. Towards the tree I was hiding behind. And I just swung. I swung my arm. My fist closed as tight as I could close it. I heard the slap. Then I felt it. Up and down my arm.

My heart is starting to burn, too, so I grab onto a tree, and swing around it, to stop. And to hide. And to steady my breathing and rub at my chest. Then I move my head so I can peek around the tree and through the forest. I don't know where it is from here that I left him lying on his back. I don't even know if he is still on his back. Maybe he is back to his feet already. He may not be that far behind me. I look in every direction. And now I don't know if I am running towards him, or away from him. So, I lean my back into a tree to steady my breathing, trying to be as quiet as I can be. And as hidden as I can be. And while I am leaning against the tree I hold my eyes closed, and I listen... I listen for him... For the sound of anybody moving. But all I can hear are the crows above. Flapping. And cawking. Suddenly, I hear a swoosh. In the distance. The swoosh of tyres. Tyres of a car. So I hold my eyes closed even tighter... Until I hear another swoosh, and my finger points.

When I open my eyes, I follow my finger. Towards the sound of those swooshes. Towards the sound of a road.

And as I begin to walk faster, I shake my arm out again, because the pain is shooting up and down it, then I hold it tight to my side and I begin to pick up my pace... jogging, then running...

I hear a creak, suddenly. Somewhere behind me, and I dive to the twigs behind a tree. In the quiet, I hear my heart begin to thump. Loud. And fast. That creak sounded close... Really close. Maybe the man in the ugly yellow jacket didn't stay down too long after I hit him. Maybe he's on my tail. There's a flap sound, that frightens me, then a large crow takes off from the forest ground, slapping through the branches as it rises... and rises.. eventually disappearing into the mist above.

'Kurva!' I say, swearing at the crow. Then I laugh. I laugh into the twigs.

That's when it hits me. The pain. Not the burn from the running. Or the bone in my arm. It's the guilt in my stomach. I didn't mean to take them. Honest to God in that grey sky above, I didn't mean to take them. It wasn't planned. Today wasn't supposed to be the day. No day was supposed to be the day. Not really. It just... it just happened. It was too easy. Sofie walked towards me... right into my hands...

I shake my head again while I am still lying on the twigs, to rid Sofie's pretty little face from my mind, then I sit up and pat at the satchel on my back, thinking of the new life the money will bring me, so I don't have to think about Sofie. This money will give me a life. Soon. As soon as I can get out of this hell. Out of this forest.

I push back to my feet, then brush myself down before I tighten the straps of the satchel against my shoulders. When I stand upright, I close my eyes to listen... listen for that swoosh again... For the sound of the road. It takes its time. But a car finally passes. A loud swoosh. Louder than the last swishes. I'm close. Closer than I was.

I walk towards the sound of the tyres, then I begin to run.... Faster. And faster. In between the trees until another swoosh, a louder swoosh, tells me I'm almost there. And then I am there. On the edge of the forest. From where I can see it. The grey concrete of a road. A road that will take me out of this hell.

A red car swooshes past as I slide down the embankment. And when my feet touch the road I look up and down it. It's empty... empty for now... But I hear them before I see them. The tyres. Tyres coming my way. So, I hold my arms above my head and begin to wave....

'Stop! Stop! Stop!' I shout. 'Stop!'

The car skids, then screeches to a stop in front of me.

'Dekuji, dekuji,' I call out, slapping my hand against the bonnet. 'Dekuji.'

I slap my hands closed together as if I am praying at the driver who is looking at me as if I have three heads. But when I knock on his side window, he winds it down.

'Potrbuji vytah,' I say. 'Prosim. Prosim.' I press my hands tighter together as I beg. 'Please. Please.'

He nods before stretching across the passenger seat of his car and snatching the door open.

And as I pull it wider open, I smile. That didn't take long. Getting out of this hell.

'Hey!' a voice shouts.

I look up and down the road in search of the shout. But I can't see it... I can't see anyone.

'Hey!'

Louder this time.

Then I see it, that ugly yellow jacket calling at me from the edge of the forest.

'Hey! Horata!' he shouts.

I drop into the passenger seat of the car, then slam the door closed, causing the pain to shoot up my arm again. And when I spin around, the driver is staring at me as if I have four heads this time.

'Jit! Jit! Jit!' I say to him, grabbing my arm.

But he just sits there. Staring at me. So, I stretch across him, and snatch open his door before lifting my feet up to kick at him, kicking him out of his own car.

LENNY

17:35

Lenny's body lays flat on the forest bed, the cawking from the crows high above not loud enough to bring him round.

His bottom lip is bloodied, and his mouth is wide open, sucking a gurgle to the back of his throat—the only sign of life within him... Until one eye eventually blinks, then both eyes begin to blink. Rapidly.

He scatters across the forest bed like a cat upon waking, kicking up twigs and dust. Then he immediately holds two fingers to his chin, before staring at sticky blood.

'Ouch,' he says.

A creak snaps in the distance and his head pivots, and his eyes dart between the thousands of tall grey trunks around him. But the forest falls silent again, but for the cawking of the German crows high above.

'Ouch, he says again, sucking air in through his teeth, the cut on his chin stinging.

He pushes himself to his feet, his head whoozing and dizzying. The trunks of the trees pulsing in and out—slowly in and out—as if they're waving at him. Beckoning him.

'Holy shit!' he says to the tree he is gripping. 'Woah!'

When he looks above, the grey sky spins as if it's warping, and the tallest branches of the trees begin to flicker and shiver.

'Shit, shit, shit!'

He closes his eyes, to rid his head of the spinning, hugging the trunk tight. And with his eyes closed, he remembers why he's here. Why he's hugging a tree in the middle of a grey, misty forest. He recalls the car crash. Running towards the forest. Running in the forest. Hearing a crow. Hearing somebody running. Then, slap. Black!

'Bastard caught me,' he whispers to the tree as he holds fingers to his chin again.

He steadies his breathing before blinking his eyes open, to find himself staring upwards, hopeful the sky has stopped spinning. But it hasn't. So, he sighs out loud as Sofie's pretty little face smiles at him through the grey above.

'I've gotta catch this mother fucker,' he reminds himself.

He unwraps one arm from the tree, then, more tentatively, the other before balancing on his two feet.

'Stay focused,' he whispers.

He places one foot in front of the other, and when his fingertips leave the bark, he steps forward on his own, the twigs crunching under his pointed black leather shoes, his mind blurring and whirring.

He dives his hand into the deep pocket of his yellow jacket, to check his phone. He hasn't missed any activity. Not in all the time he was lying flat out on the bed of the forest. Whatever amount of time that was. He's not sure. So, he checks the time on his phone—17:39—then shakes his head. He can't have been flat out for long. He might still be on the tail of Horata. Which wouldn't be so bad, if Lenny's head wasn't spinning, and the twigs weren't flickering different colours on the forest bed.

He chicanes between the trees, his fingers brushing against them for support, his head darting left, and then right, over each of his shoulders. He has no idea if he's walking in the right direction. No idea what direction he's walking in at all... when suddenly he hears a familiar sound. Tyres. Screeching to a stop.

His head darts left, then his pace quickens, his fingers still brushing trees as he jogs past them and around them. Suddenly, he's racing, his head spinning, the trees he's chicaning waving at him as he passes them. He huffs and puffs, squinting through the greyness ahead. Until he sees it in the gap of the tall trunks. A grey road.

He sprints towards it and when he arrives at the forest's edge, his head throbbing, he has to grab hold of a tree for balance. For support. He stares down the embankment that leads to the grey road, then creeps his head out from behind the final row of trees. That's when he sees him. Horata. Talking to somebody in a car.

'Hey!' Lenny shouts, his head still swaying.

When he steps foot onto the edge of the muddy hill that leads to the road, the earth crumbles beneath him, and he tumbles, head over feet. Then feet over head. Until his tail bone crashes to the concrete below.

'Hey!' he shouts again.

'Holy shit,' he mumbles to himself, his head swaying, the embankment pulsating a multitude of brown shades at him.

'Horata!' he shouts. Weakly. Because he barely has the strength to speak, let alone shout.

He slowly gets to his feet, then begins to shuffle his way towards the car Horata got in. But it suddenly speeds off, bellowing road dust back at him.

'Fuck!' he shouts, bending forward, his hands clutching his knees, heaving heavy breaths to his lungs.

'Ahoj,' a strange voice says.

Lenny's brow dips as a heavy-set man with an oversized moustache appears out of the dust cloud.

'English?' Lenny asks, squinting.

'What is going on?' the rotund man asks.

'Did a man with a beard?' Lenny gasps for air. 'I need to sit,' he says, unzipping his yellow jacket. 'I need to sit.'

He staggers to the other side of the road, to where he rests a shoulder against the muddied embankment.

'What is going on!?' the rotund man asks. 'Who are you?'

Lenny breathes heavily, then looks up from his slouched position at the irate man in front of him.

'Did a man with a beard steal your car?'

'Yes,' the rotund man says. 'He kicked me out of my Skoda.'

'Hold on, hold on,' Lenny says showing the man his palm. He closes his eyes, takes three steady breaths, then stands back upright, leaning off the embankment.

'Don't worry, sir,' he says. 'We're going to track that man down.'

Lenny steps to the centre of the road and holds his palm out, waiting on the next car to come his way.

'Do you know that bastard?' the rotund man asks, following him. 'The bastard with the beard?'

'I do, sir,' Lenny says. 'His name is Javi Horata. And I promise you, sir. We're going to track him down.'

Lenny stands motionless in the centre of the road his hand still outstretched as the rotund man circles him, staring at him.

'Who is Javi Horata?' he asks.

'Now that is,' Lenny says, before he hears the woosh of tyres coming their way, 'a long story.'

Lenny stands brave as the car speeds towards him causing it to screech to a halt.

'I'm sorry,' Lenny says, tapping at the bonnet. 'My name is Lenny Moon. I am a private investigator and I need your help.'

'Vot?' a shocked, bespectacled man shouts, winding down his window.

'I need your help,' Lenny repeats.

He snatches the passenger door open and worms his way inside the vehicle without invitation.

'I need you to catch the car in front of us,' he says. 'It has about a two-minute head start. But you will be helping the law, sir. Please... let's go!'

The man stares though his bottle-thick lenses at Lenny's cut chin then up into the investigator's eyes, before the back of the car sinks.

'I'm coming too,' the rotund man says, slapping the back door closed, his knees up tight against the two chairs in front of him.

'This man just had his car stolen,' Lenny says. 'Let's go... let's go...'

Lenny rolls his fingers over and over, signalling to the driver that he needs to step on the pedal. Quickly.

'What is going on?' the driver says, fixing his thick glasses on the bridge of his nose.

'Move!' the rotund man shouts from the back seat.

The bespectacled man jolts from the boom, then pushes the gear stick into first, and slowly steps on the gas pedal.

'Quicker!' Lenny and the rotund man roar in unison.

SOFIE

The rocking slows before the noise of the engine stops. Then everything goes still. And steady. And silent. The only noise is the boat gently rocking on the river.

I wipe my eyes into my shoulder, then I sit up for the first time since I lay on top of my Kindle, just so I can peek over the rim of the boat. It's quiet around here. So, so quiet. A bit like Vlatva and Labe was quiet before the sirens came. The difference here is the fields aren't yellow. They're brown. Same brown as the leaves on the trees.

I feel for the Kindle with my fingers and try to pinch it. But I can't lift it with my hands tied behind my back. Not before he walks towards me and stands over me. When I look up, I see that his hair looks all blown out like Philomena's back in the orphanage. And he looks just as angry as she always looks.

'Keep your head down,' he says.

He coughs. Then he leans over me, stretching his arm over the side of the boat.

'You got the cargo?' another voice asks.

'You got the one-hundred thousand?'

I look up to see the long-haired man grabbing a small bag. A small bag he looks inside before he throws it over his shoulder, and it lands across from me on the other side of the speedboat with a thump. One hundred thousand doesn't look as big as it sounds.

'Up!' the long-haired man says, as I am staring at the bag. He grabs under both arms and lifts me. And as he lifts, I try to pinch the Kindle. I scratch and scrape for it. But it drops. And lands by his big feet.

'Nooo!' I say, as the other man's hands come under my arms, lifting me away from the boat. 'Noooo! Please.'

'Shut up,' the new man says, squeezing the back of my neck. Then moving his big, round nose towards my face.

So, I do. I shut up and stare at him.

'How old's this?' he asks.

'Seven,' the long-haired man says.

'Eight,' I say.

'Do you have tape? To put across her mouth?' he asks.

'I won't speak. I won't make any more noise,' I say. 'I promise. If I could... if I could have my Kindle.' I nod over the rim of the boat, and the long-haired man looks down. 'If I'm reading, I'll say nothing. I'll just read. I promise.'

The long-haired man bends and picks up my Kindle, twisting and turning it in his giant, hairy hand.

'I got my money. It's up to you?' he says to the man still holding my neck. The one with the big, round nose.

'Vot is it?' he asks.

'Kindle, correct?' the long-haired man asks me.

I nod. I just nod. I don't say anything.

'Just books, huh?' Big, Round Nose asks.

I nod again. And so does the man with the long hair. Then the man with the round nose takes the Kindle from his hairy hand and drags me away from the boat by the back of my neck.

As he is pushing me through the muddy field, the speedboat makes that ugly noise again behind us and takes off.

I look around at it speeding back down the river, then up at Big, Round Nose, to see if he might be nice. If his eyes might be nice.

'Mister,' I say, 'Can you untie my hands?'

'No,' he says.

'I will be able to hold the Kindle for you.'

He stops walking, and holds a hand to my chest, putting his big, round nose close to my small, skinny nose.

'Girl, shut up!'

'Where are you taking me?'

'Girl, shut up!'

I stare up at him, then he drags me along again, through the muddy field. And my mind starts thinking. And thinking. Too fast. Way too fast. Too fast I don't know what to think. I have so many questions. So, so many. But I can't ask any. Not with him telling me to shut up and dragging me by the back of the neck.

As he is dragging me, I stare at the Kindle in his hand, and I know I have to get it from him. That is the only way I can be saved. I have to text private investigator Lenny Moon. And give him clues to where I am. Where I'm going to.

I look around. To see if there are any clues I can text when I get my Kindle back in my hands. But there's no clues around here. Just brown, muddy fields. And brown, sad trees.

'Where are we going?' I whisper. Really quietly. So he doesn't shout at me or grab my neck tighter.

'You speak good English, yes?' he asks.

'Yes,' I say, nodding.

'Vell then you understand vot 'shut up' means, yes?'

I look away, him still dragging my neck, his knuckles digging harder into me, my wrists stinging behind my back, my legs jogging fast to keep up. I start shivering. Again. From the fright. And from the cold.

'Tu es une fille tellement stupide, Sofie,' I whisper to myself.

I *am* so stupid. I shouldn't have walked so far away from the orphanage this morning. I shouldn't have walked that far into the fields.

'We're here,' he says.

When I look up, I see a white van parked next to an iron gate at the end of the field ahead. And I know he is dragging me towards it.

'What's in there?' I ask.

I can hear, when I say that, that my voice is shivering as much as my body.

'Shut up!' he says. Again. It's all he says.

As we get nearer I see that the registration on the back of the van is from Poland. It has POL by the European flag. The long-haired man must have brought me all the way to Poland on the speedboat. I see the letters R and K on the registration, but I don't see the numbers that follow them. Not before he swings me around, lifts me, and then throws me hard into the side of the van. No seats. No nothing. Just dirty white metal. All around me. Then he slides the door closed. And everything goes dark.

JAVI

This car is a lot faster than the heavy blue car I've been driving around in for the last three weeks. It whizzes as if it is hovering above the road. I can't feel any bumps. Or dips. It's like being on a train. And it's warm. Very warm. And I'm never warm. It would be nice to take this car all the way to wherever it is I start my new life. I could steal some licence plates along the way. Put them over the plates on this car... But that's probably a dangerous game to play now. Now that they know what I'm driving away in. I'll have to change the car at some point. But that is no problem to me. I'm used to changing cars. I've been driving around in stolen cars since I got out of prison. Since before I even went to prison. Old cars. The type nobody really cares to investigate much. The ones I know I just have to change a number plate on, and I can get away with driving it until it breaks down. Then I sell the parts for some money. And steal a different old car. I have stolen three cars since I got out of prison eighteen months ago. But I have never driven a brand-new car like this one. One that hovers.

I look between the steering wheel at the petrol gauge. Half a tank. That should get me out of the Czech Republic anyway. I'll make a decision on changing the car after I cross the border.

I glance up to the rear-view mirror to make sure I'm not being followed. If it took me seconds to get a driver to stop, it won't take yellow jacket long to get a driver to stop, too. Especially if he has a badge. He must be a cop. He arrived at Vlatva and Labe in a police car anyway. Or some smart black BMW with a blue siren flashing anyway. I bet he's not a regular police officer. Probably Interpol. Or something important like that. I need to make distance from him. As quick as I can.

I start to tap at the steering wheel as the car hovers above the road and as my fingers are tapping, I decide to tug the steering wheel left, to drive through the yellow field instead of taking the road. I have got to shake him off, just in case he's already stopped the next car and is chasing me.

I have no idea what direction I'm driving in across this field. I delivered my cargo to Vlatva and Labe. Drove north away from there before Ugly Yellow Jacket crashed into me. Ran through a forest east of the river. Then, I ended up stealing this car on some narrow road that could be anywhere in any direction... I have no idea what direction I exited the forest from. I have no idea what direction I'm driving in now across this yellow field...

I blow out my cheeks as the car no longer feels as if it is hovering but struggling through the grass. I'll just have to find the next road at the end of this field. Then I'll be away from whoever's behind me. I'll be on the road that will lead me to my new life.

The car shakes and crunches a bit more, but suddenly the grass is not so long, and I am gliding through the field. Speeding through the field. Ahead, I see the grass is turning green. And I feel I must be heading in the direction of Prague. Back to the city I thought I'd left for the final time this morning. So, I go cross-eyed as my brain adds up the map in my head. If Prague is straight ahead and I want to go north-west of Prague towards western Europe I should be.... I tug the car right, aware I will be going back on myself a little. But this is the direction I need to be going in. To get out of the Czech Republic. To go towards western Europe. Towards Portugal. Or Spain. Or France. Or wherever I end up moving to with my fifty-thousand euro.

When my fingers tap against the steering wheel I know I am being nervous. But like Sofie and Liam's faces, I just have to put my nerves to the back of my mind. I need to just think about getting out of here. Getting free. Getting my new life started.

I swivel my head over my shoulder again as the car struggles through the long grass to stare at the satchel in the back seat before turning back to squint through the sea of yellow ahead of me. Fifty-thousand euro will be enough. It will be enough rent for as long as it takes for me to get a job. I'm going to buy some nice clothes. Get myself into the nice bars, talking to nice people, then say I'm a barman myself. If I look good, they'll trust me. They'll trust me enough to offer me some work. I'm sure I'll get work if I look good. If I look like I already have money.

As the top of the longest grass taps against the windows, the pain I had almost forgotten about shoots up my right arm again. And as I am squeezing my fingers in and out to try to stop the pain, my head suddenly swings to the left, noticing a slither of grey amongst all of the yellow. It's a slither of grey I have seen before. I know what it is. Even from this distance. Klay Bridge. The bridge that will take me to the E Road, the E Road that stretches west... all the way to Germany. That's the road that will set me free.

LENNY

17:52

The rotund man leans forward and farts—a squeaky trombone honking behind him just before he wraps his arms around the two front seats.

Lenny, already frustrated, huffs before opening the passenger window a crack, horrified by the potential stench.

'Oi,' the rotund man says from behind as his hand lands on Lenny's shoulder. 'Your jacket is wet, no?'

Lenny huffs again, and his head bows.

'It's a long story,' he mopes. Then he glances at the driver. 'Can't you go quicker?'

The driver steps firmer on the gas, but the engine only growls as they go in chase of the stolen Skoda ahead. Somewhere, anywhere ahead.

'That bastard kicked me five times with both feet,' the rotund man says.

'Believe you me he has done worse things than that,' Lenny replies.

'What he do?' the driver asks.

'I can't say.'

'Did he do that to your face?'

Lenny feels at his chin again. But when he takes his fingers away there is no wet blood this time. It has, by now, all dried to his stubble.

'He did.'

Lenny rests his forehead into the palm of his hand and attempts to massage the spinning. Then he shifts uncomfortably in his heavy, damp clothes, pulling at the neck of his shirt.

'Are you good, my friend?' the driver asks.

'Is it hot. Or just me?' Lenny replies, pulling at his collar again. He is trying to shuffle his arms out of the sleeves of his puffer jacket when his head suddenly thumps against the side window, and his cheek slides down it.

The rotund man leans forward again, another trumpet of fart honking from him.

'Is he dead?' he asks the driver.

The driver stretches a hand to Lenny's neck, feeling for a pulse.

'No. He just fainted. Vot is going on?'

The rotund man wraps his arms around the driver's seat and breathes heavily into his ear from behind.

'I was driving and a man with a beard waved me down. He got inside my car, then he is kicking me out of my car. With both feet. Bastard.'

'And then?'

'This man here.' He slaps Lenny on the shoulder. 'Was chasing the man with the beard, I think. He waved you down... now here we are. The three of us. Chasing, in your car, after my car.'

The driver refixes the glasses on the bridge of his nose as he continues to speed through the narrow country road.

'Who is this guy?' He points his thumb towards Lenny slunk

into the passenger side of his car, his mouth slightly ajar, his head lightly vibrating against the cold window.

'He works for the, uh,' the rotund man sits back, his heavy brow dipping. 'What is it again? The TUP? TUB? BUT? No, I would have remembered if he worked for BUT.'

'Is he police?' the driver asks glancing at the rear-view mirror to see the rotund man sitting in the backseat of his family car shrugging his wide shoulders.

'I don't know,' the rotund man says.

'Hey, man,' the driver rubs at Lenny's chest. Hard. 'Wake up!'

Lenny snorts and heaves, before sinking down the passenger seat, his eyes firmly shut, a snore gurgling in the back of his throat.

'Wake up!' the rotund man shouts.

He reaches forward and rubs a tubby hand over Lenny's face.

'Wake up British man,' he says. 'Wake up!'

Lenny snorts again, then sits bolt upright before staring at the driver, his eyes blinking rapidly. He darts his confused face over his shoulder, to be met by the short, rotund man with the moustache he recalls appeared out of a dust cloud on the roadside.

'Holy shit,' Lenny says, sucking heavy breaths in and out of his dry mouth. He pats down himself, feeling the damp. The damp from the river. The river he dived into. And he engulfs himself in it again, the slap against the cold, choppy water. Then the punch of the Air Bag as it exploded in his face. The clatter of a closed fist against his chin.

'Ouch!' Lenny says, holding fingers below his lips again.

'You good, my friend?' the driver asks.

'I...I, uh. I think so. We need to... we need to—'

'You work for the TUB?' the driver asks, refixing his glasses.

'What? No... I work for the, watch out!' Lenny screams at the driver as a car speeds towards them. The driver pulls onto the right side of the road, then holds a hand up to his passengers after a yellow car zooms by, its horn trumpeting.

'You're an officer, yes?'

'An investigator.'

The driver glances in the rear-view mirror at the rotund man, to see his backseat passenger now lost in his phone, scrolling.

'Fuck!' the rotund man says, leaning forward again, a loud prrrttt darting from his backside again. Louder than the last two. He doesn't notice his flatulence. Or care to notice it. 'I just remembered. Where's My Car?'

Lenny looks around, his brow dipped.

'That's what we're trying to find.'

'No. Where's My Car? The app. The app on my phone, I can track it. I can track my car.'

Lenny's eyes light up.

'You have the Where's My Car app?'

'Yes,' the rotund man says, thumbing his phone, his tongue hanging out of his mouth.

'Hold on... hold on.' He holds up a finger. 'My car is... my car is... Wait... Where is it? I'm no good with maps.'

His eyebrows sink and he hands the phone to Lenny who takes it from him before rubbing at the centre of his forehead—attempting to stem the dizziness. Then he blows out a cool exhale before studying the map on the screen.

'He's coming back on himself,' Lenny says, excitedly. 'He's heading for the E Road. We can get there before him. Take the next turn right towards the that bridge. He's just driving out of those fields over there... In about four minutes he'll be driving over that bridge. We can get there before him.'

The driver nods once, and then Lenny turns around to the rotund man, offering half a smile.

'I almost forgot,' the rotund man says, cackling a heavy laugh. 'Where's My Car. I remember thinking when the man who sold me the car insisted I download the app 'why would I ever lose my car?' Now here we are. The three of us. Looking for my car. My name is Yuri.'

'Nice to meet you Yuri,' Lenny says.

As Lenny stretches his hand over his shoulder towards the rotund man in the back seat, the car suddenly yanks to the right and begins stuttering.

'Let's take a short cut,' the driver calls out.

The car rattles and shakes through the yellow field, heading straight toward the only concrete cutting through the line on the horizon. The Klay Bridge.

Lenny blows a heavy exhale, then presses the tips of fingers to his brow, his head threatening to spin again, a sharp whooze engulfing him.

'Are you good, man? You look...' the rotund man leaves his question there and leans back in his seat again.

'I'm grand, yeah. It's just... I've been chasing this bastard all day.'

The car crunches under them as it lifts back on to a smooth country road, then it speeds off, aiming straight for the tall bridge in the distance.

'Okay,' Lenny says staring at the rotund man's phone. 'We're almost there. He's about a minute behind us. But he is one hundred percent heading for that bridge. Let's park lengthways across it. It'll block him off totally. Then we'll get this bastard behind bars.'

'Then we will get my car back,' the rotund man says.

Lenny pinches at his temples and closes his eyes as the car zooms towards the bridge and when he opens them, they're already there. They've already reached their destination.

'Okay,' he instructs the driver. 'Turn around. Side on. Leave no room for him to cross.'

'But I don't want him to crash my car. I don't want any damage...' the driver says.

'He won't crash into it,' Lenny assures him. 'He'll have to stop. He'll have no choice but to stop.'

The driver pulls over, then three-point turns so that his car sits neatly across the entrance of the bridge, a bridge that leads to western Europe.

'Okay,' Lenny says squinting at the screen in front of him, 'He's narrowing in. He's coming this way... One thousand metres...'

The three men stare out of the left-side of the car, their eyes wide, their expectation uncertain.

'Five hundred metres...'

The Skoda appears as a dot on the horizon, heading straight towards them at full speed, until it gets bigger, and bigger. And faster and faster.

'Shit,' Lenny says, his eyes widening. 'He's not stopping!'

BETSY

I feel good. Really good. Really, really good. Not scared. Not scared like I used to feel when there were this many people around me.

This is the second time this week I've taken the tram into and out of the city centre. To do some shopping. Shopping for my new house.

The first time I was a little scared. But today, I feel nothing. I only feel good. Happy. Happy sitting around other people. I don't talk to them. Or look at them. I just keep my head down, staring at the floor of the tram where it spins and twists. But I don't mind being around them. Or them being around me. Not anymore.

When I stand, a young man moves his knee out of my way, so I can walk past him.

'Sorry,' he whispers.

'No problem,' I whisper back, glancing at him. His smile makes me smile. And then I step toward the double doors and stare out through them, waiting on the tram to stop. When it does, I press at the button that will sweep the doors open and when I step into the cold, I spin around, to see he is still smiling at me. I stand staring at him, until the doors sweep closed, and the tram takes off, its bell ringing as it picks up speed.

I grip the bag tighter in my hand and begin walking over the bridge. The bridge that leads towards my new house. My new home. And as I walk, I wonder who the young man on the tram is. What his name is. What he's like. If he's kind. Or polite. If he reads a lot like I do. Maybe we have lots in common. But I'll never know. Because the young man on the Luas is in the distance now. Already over the bridge at the far end of the canal, speeding in a straight line towards Inchicore.

Maybe I should give him a name. Like Clayton. Or Neville. Or maybe something more Mediterranean. Spanish. Javi. That's a nice name. The nice name of a nice-looking man.

Then I shake my head of the character I just made up. I don't need a boyfriend. I've never needed a boyfriend. And even though lots of boyfriends and girlfriends fall in love forever in the books I read, I bet real life isn't like that. I bet most women don't get swept off their feet by a handsome man from the nineteenth century. I bet most marriages are bit like my Mom and Dad's. Couples who don't like to be in the same room as each other.

So, I shake my head of the young man on the tram and grip my bag tighter as I cross the road towards my new house. Towards my basement. Betsy's basement.

As soon as I turn the key in the door, like real adults do, I can smell home. I can smell me. I can smell the safety this home brings. Especially when I slam the door behind me, shutting out the world.

I kick my shoes off, landing them at the bottom step, then I drop my shopping bag and shake my coat from my arms before hanging it on the square of the newel of the bannisters. Jane Austen taught me what a newel was.

It's warm in here. Really, really warm. And it makes me think that maybe I should take Mom's advice to not have the heating on all of the time. Especially when I'm not even home. She moaned all last week when she was here that the house was too hot. But if it wasn't the heating, she'd moan about something else. Probably Dad. Dad and Winnie. Winnie the Witch as Mom calls her. I just did what I usually do when Mom is talking. I pretended to be listening to the conversation while I was thinking about different things. Like stories. Or books. Or characters. Nodding and shaking my head when I knew she required my input.

I sweep the shopping up off the brown floorboards of my hallway and step towards the gold knob on the door that leads to my basement. I always feel happy when I open this door, and every time I am walking down these steps I smile. I smile because I know I am home. I know I am safe. Safe as can be.

I can still sense him down here. Hear him. Smell him. And I wonder if the young man on the tram is like Dod. If he is, maybe he could have been my boyfriend. A younger Dod, of course. But somebody who was kind like Dod was kind. And caring like Dod cared. And who made me laugh like Dod made me laugh. Nobody since I got found has made me laugh the way Dod made me laugh. I miss it. I miss laughing.

'You don't need a boyfriend, Betsy,' I remind myself out loud as I am shaking the white box out of the shopping bag.

I rest the box onto my desk while tossing the bag onto my new bed, then I stab my long thumb nail into the tape on each side of the cardboard, snapping the lid open.

When I lift the lid I immediately rub at it. Because it looks so smooth and so shiny and so new. And then I take it out, pushing the empty box it came in to one side.

I place it on the desk, then rub at the top of it again, feeling the smooth, cold metal before I sit myself into the chair and push myself closer to the desk. When I lift the top open a noise beeps from the speakers, like a piano playing two loud chords. It frightens me. Then I smile. And as the screen blinks on, I rub my hands. Excited. I don't know why I'm excited. I've no idea what I'm going to do next. Or even how I'm going to do it. I just know it's a great opportunity for me. A different opportunity.

It was all Monica's idea. My agent. She watched me while we were promoting Betsy's Basement, reading, reading, and reading as we travelled in cars and trains and planes.

'You should write fiction,' she told me.

'Me?' I said. I was shocked. Really, really shocked.

I'd never even thought of it. I'm still not sure it's a great idea. Even now. Even as this laptop blinks to life. But I sure am going to give it a go.

JAVI

I have never been in a car crash. Not until today. Now I have been in two. Two within the time of one hour.

The pain in my right arm was sore before this crash. From slapping the man in the ugly yellow coat across the face. But now it's more than really painful. It is as if I broke a bone when I smashed into that car. I think my right shoulder hit the steering wheel before the Air Bag exploded. I just remember moving the Air Bag out of my way, then reaching for the handle to push open the door.

That's where I am now. Standing on the concrete, my right arm hanging by my side. Broken. Definitely broken. But I run. I run as fast as I can with one good arm.

Suddenly the concrete is coming towards me. And it stings. It stings my cheek. And I breathe heavily, before spitting something hard out of my mouth. When it skids across the concrete, I see that it is my tooth. Suddenly legs are running towards me. Loads of legs. Six legs.

'Get the fuck down, get that fuckin' head down!' a man roars into the back of my head. His body lands on mine. His arm digging hard into my neck. Then a second set of legs arrive, and my face is shoved to the ground, scraping against the concrete.

'Javi Horata, you are under arrest,' another man shouts into my ear.

I scrape my face against the ground to look around, and I see that it is him. The man in the ugly yellow jacket. Celtic accent. Probably Scottish. Welsh. Irish. One of those kind.

'You owe me a brand-new car!' another accent says, before a blow lands on the back of my head. My cheek smacks the concrete and, in shock, I roll over, sweeping whoever it is lying on my back away from me.

'Hold on, hold on, hold on,' I say as his fist balls, about to swing at me. 'My arm is broken. My arm is broken. I cannot fight. You are beating a helpless man!'

I breathe heavy as I sit up, seeing three faces staring down at me.

'You weren't helpless when you were kicking me out of my own car,' the fat one says. He lifts his foot. And slams it into my face. The sting from the sole of his shoe hurts more than my broken arm. And I roll back, my head smacking against the concrete. Caught. Caught for kidnapping two children. I'm going back behind bars. For a long stretch this time. For the rest of the best years of my life.

'Roll the fuck over,' the Celtic accent says. He grabs me and turns me over. 'My name is Investigator Lenny Moon with the PTU. You, you little scumbag are under arrest for the kidnapping and trafficking of two minors.'

'Wait? This man kidnaps children?' one of the men asks.

'I did not mean to take them,' I say. 'Honest to God above, I never meant to take them.'

Investigator Lenny Moon huffs in his ugly yellow jacket, then he spins away from us, holding his phone to his ear.

The other two men look at each other, then down at me.

'You owe me a new fucking car, you paedophile!' the fat one says.

He holds his fist into a ball again...

'Yes. Yes. Yes. Yes,' I say. 'Look it's all insured. Once he,' I nod towards the ugly yellow jacket talking on the phone behind them, 'arrests me then your insurance will pay out. You'll get a brand-new car. I'll be charged with the theft of your car and the... and the...'

I can't breathe anymore.

'You kidnap kids?' the other accent says. I know it's a local accent speaking English. Broken English like my English.

While the two men stand over me asking different questions, I try to think. I try to think my way out of it.

'Listen to me,' I say, 'he is with the PTU. He will be able to make sure everything is... Wait, what is the PTU?' I ask.

'Yeah, what is the PTU?' the fat man asks the other man.

'PTU? No idea,' the man with the local accent says, shaking his head. We're all shaking our heads when the ugly yellow jacket turns around and walks back towards us.

'You,' I say, sitting up. 'What is the PTU?'

'The PTU?' yellow jacket says. 'The People Trafficking Unit.'

'Never heard of it,' the fat man says.

'Yeah, never heard of it,' I say. 'You got a badge?'

He shakes his little bald head.

'I don't, actually,' he says.

LENNY

18:18

Lenny presses the phone to his ear with one hand while the other massages the crown of his bald head.

'Are you okay, Lenny Moon?' she says. 'You sound a bit slow. Stuttery.'

'Olette,' he replies, exasperated, 'You wouldn't believe what I've been through. Just please tell me,' he pauses to steady his breathing, 'how long till you get here?'

'Our man is fourteen minutes out,' she informs him.

'Quick as he can,' Lenny huffs.

He bows his head as he hangs up the call, then spins around to see the rotund man and the bespectacled man standing over Horata. He shovels the phone into his pocket, holds his hands to his hips and blows out a deep exhale as he strides towards them.

'You,' Horata shouts out as Lenny approaches. 'What is the PTU?'

Lenny blinks his eyes rapidly at the concrete beneath him as it pulsates a variety of colours at him.

'The PTU,' he says. 'The People Trafficking Unit.'

'Never heard of it,' the rotund man says.

'Yeah, never heard of it,' Horata says. 'You got a badge?'

Lenny lifts his stare from the pulsating concrete and squints across the concrete bridge, at nothing in the distance.

'I don't, actually,' he says.

The two men glare at him. Blankly. As if he's the suspicious one, and not the bearded trafficker sitting by their feet.

'What in hell is going on here?' the rotund man says. 'I'm ringing the police. The proper police.'

He spins, struggling to retrieve his phone from his tight jeans pocket.

'No, no, don't call the police...' Lenny says, but his voice tails off as the rotund man lifts his phone to his ear. Lenny bows his head, the pulsating matching the throbbing.

'Are you okay, friend?' the bespectacled man asks.

'I.. I,' Lenny stutters before pausing. Then he sweeps his feet forward and lands his bony ass to the concrete, bowing his head again to stem the swaying.

'You. PTU guy, are you okay?'

The bespectacled man rubs at Lenny's shoulder.

'Yeah, yeah,' Lenny says, 'I'm fine. I'm just—

Suddenly Horata takes off, scooting himself to his feet and sprinting as fast as he can, the satchel bouncing on his back as he races toward the bridge.

The bespectacled man takes after him, but Lenny remains sitting in a slump, both hands over his face, lost in a haze of blurs.

'And he's trying to get away now!' the rotund man shouts into his phone before he begins to give chase, too. 'So get here as quick as you can!'

He huffs and puffs as he runs, stuffing his phone back into his jeans pocket, and as Lenny's hands slowly slip from his face and he blinks his eyes back open, he is sure he is watching the bespectacled man wrestling Horata to the ground, then the rotund man diving on top of both of them.

'What the fuck is going on?' Lenny mutters, slapping both of his cheeks. But instead of waking up, he slumps to another sleep, his eyes closing, the back of his head thumping to the concrete. As he lays flat across the foot of the bridge, in the shadow of two smashed cars, his mouth opens and closes repeatedly, as if parched.

'Celina,' he whispers. 'Celina.'

He smiles. Wide. Then Celina smiles back at him, her left eyebrow dipping as if smiling is naughty to her. He loves when her left eyebrow dips.

'They're in the garden, Len-ny,' she says. 'A drink?'

'Red wine,' he mouths. 'Be lovely.'

He cranes his neck to stare through the open kitchen doors at Jared and Jacob chasing each other in a circle, the grass a lucid green, the pale sky cloudless and stark.

'Here,' she says, holding a glass of red towards him.

'Thank you,' he says, pinching the stem.

Celina inches to her tip-toes to kiss him where the corner of his lips meet his cheek, and Lenny inhales a breath of contentment. Happiness. Fulfilment.

'How was your morning?' she asks.

'Took a long walk through the fields...'

Celina's smile is almost as bright as the daylight flooding in from the open double doors that lead to the fresh Belgian countryside the twins are revelling in. Lenny places his glass of wine onto the large kitchen island and then holds his hands either side of Celina's pretty face. Her eyes look heavy. Heavy with lust. And he can't help himself. He inches his lips towards hers when, behind her, he notices Jared and Jacob on top of each other, trading blow after blow. Punch after punch.

'No, no, no,' he roars.

He releases his hands from Celina's face and sprints, pacing past the kitchen island and out through the double doors to where he grabs both of them by the collar.

'Get fucking off him!' Lenny screams.

When they stand back up, Lenny glares at both of them; the bespectacled man looking apologetic, the rotund man eager to land more blows.

Lenny shakes his head, then leans down to Horata's body heavy and limp on the concrete.

'Where is she? Where is Sofie Le Saux?' Lenny screams, grabbing Horata by the collar and shaking him.

'No, no, no,' Horata says. 'My arm. My arm is broken.'

'Where is she?' Lenny shouts again, shaking him even more.

'Stop,' Horata roars. 'It's hurting. Hurting.'

Lenny lets go, and Horata's shoulders thump to the concrete.

'Where is she Horata? Where the fuck has Sofie Le Saux been taken to?'

'I don't know,' Horata huffs, wiping blood from his lip. 'I don't know anything.'

Lenny presses both palms to his own temples, quelling the throbbing, stemming the pulsating.

'Don't worry,' the rotund man says. 'The proper police are on their way. He'll answer their questions when they get here.'

'The.... wait, what?' Lenny says, confused. 'You called the police?'

'Correct,' the rotund man says.

'But that's.... that's...'

Lenny's head spins again. And he hears Olette's disappointed accent, furious that the systemic arm of the law will get the plaudits again for solving a case the PTU led from the outset.

With his stomach heavy, Lenny stares solemnly across the bridge, squinting into the thick mist.

'Jesus...' he whispers to himself.

Then he stares in the opposite direction, desperate to know

which siren he will hear first. The police car the bespectacled man ordered. Or the black BMW he himself ordered.

'Listen to me,' Horata says as he rolls over, dropping the satchel from his good shoulder before zipping it open. 'If you let me go before the police get here, I will give each of you ten thousand euro...'

SOFIE

When the van door slides open I have to blink my eyes so many times because of all of the light.

I don't know how long it was that I was rolling around in the back of that horrible dark and dirty van. But it was definitely a long, long time. On a long, long drive.

'Shut up,' he says.

I didn't say anything. I just sat up and blinked.

He looks just like a shadow in front of all the sunlight. A shadow that waves me towards him. So, I crawl over the dirty, hard floor on my knees and when I reach him, I look over his shoulder, searching for clues. Any clues. Any clues I can text to private investigator Lenny Moon when I get my Kindle back.

'You have my Kindle?' I ask the shadow as he reaches his hands under my arms.

'No,' he says, lifting me, then folding me over his shoulder.

'What! Wait. What?' I say, staring down at the pavement as he walks. My stomach pressed against his shoulder.

'Shut up,' he says. 'Don't make me say shut up again.'

'No,' I whisper. Angry. So, angry. So, so angry. 'Where is my Kindle? You had my Kindle.'

'It's not yours anymore,' he says.

I begin kicking my legs, thumping my knees into his chest.

'You little bitch!' he says, dropping me to the ground.

I land on my backside and both of my hands hurt. Caught between my back and the hard ground. But the pain is not more worse than the anger.

'I need my Kindle!' I shout.

He bends down and leans his big, round nose towards my tiny nose.

'Shut up. If you shout again, or try to kick me again, I will kill you.'

My chin begins to shake, because of the cold. And because of the fright. And I just nod. I nod at his big, round nose.

'Get up!' he says.

When I stand, he grips me by the arm and drags me forward. That's the first time I can see where we are. Not in a field anymore. Not a green field. Or a yellow field. Or a brown field. We're in a car park. The car park of the big factory warehouse he is dragging me to. I want to ask what it is. Where we're going. What we're doing here. What's inside that warehouse. I want to ask him lots of things. So, so many things. But I can't. Because he will kill me if I talk again.

As we get close to the door of the warehouse I see another girl walking from a different way. Younger than me. Being brought into the same warehouse by another man. I try to look at her face as I am being dragged forward. But she doesn't look back. She looks sad. Sad like me.

When we get inside I see that there are other children. Six more. No. Seven more. All with different adults. Mostly men. One woman.

He drags me by the shoulder towards a door that he kicks open with his big boot. And when he stops and lets go of my arm, I can see myself staring at myself. I look tired. And sad. Sad like the girl I saw walking in here.

He runs a tap under the mirror, then holds his hand against the water before slapping at my face, rubbing his horrible fat fingers all over my mouth and my cheeks.

'What is—'

'Shut up!' he says.

So I do. I shut up. And I just stand there in front of the mirror while he washes my face with his dirty hand.

When he finishes, he walks into another door and begins to take some toilet roll from a container, wrapping it around and around in his hand. Then the other door opens again, and I see a little girl coming in with a man. She looks at me. And nods. And I nod back at her. But we don't say anything. She was probably told to shut up or she will be killed too. Then I can't see her anymore. Because toilet roll is covering my face. Wiping and swiping at my mouth.

'That vill have to do,' the man with the big, round nose says.

Then he rolls the toilet paper up and throws it over his shoulder before pulling the door open and dragging me by my sore arm back outside. To where more children are waiting with adults. Nine of them now. Maybe this place is like an orphanage. Maybe I'm going to have friends here. When everybody stops being sad, maybe we can all be happy. All be happy together.

He drags me past the children. Some who look at me, some who are too afraid to look at me. Then we suddenly stop at a small counter. When he lets my arm go I can still feel his fingers digging into me. It's sore. So, so sore.

He begins talking to a man in a new language. And I try to listen in, to see if I can hear anything. Then I remember... I don't need to listen for clues. I don't need to look for clues either. Not anymore. Not when I don't have my Kindle. Not when I don't have private investigator Lenny Moon coming to find me. To save me. To be my friend.

I drop to my knees by the counter. And they bang hard

against the floor. But it doesn't hurt. Nothing hurts more than the pain in my tummy. The pain that my Kindle is gone. Forever.

He drags me up by the arm. Hard. Then I see him taking a ticket from the man at the counter. A ticket with the number 026 on it.

I look around to see if other adults have ticket numbers, but before I can see any I am being dragged by my sore arm across the warehouse floor again. In the other direction this time. Towards a big black curtain. A curtain he pulls across, before he drags me towards some small wooden steps. I try to look up them. To see what's up there. But it's too dark. It's too dark all around here. And quiet. So, so quiet.

While we stand in the darkness, with nobody else around us, I think he might not kill me if I talk. Because there's nobody else here.

'Can I have my Kindle? Please?' I say. Quietly.

He looks down at me. And then suddenly I hear a loud boom. Like a microphone. A voice. A different language. Definitely through a microphone. Probably Polish language. That's the only clue I have. That the registration on the back of the white van was from Poland.

The man with the big round nose squeezes my arm tight again and begins dragging me up the steps. Dragging me towards the dark. Towards the boom of the microphone. When we reach the top of the steps, I see a light ahead. A big light. Shining down at nothing. Shining down at the dirty warehouse floor below.

'Zero. Dwa. Szesc,' the microphone booms. 'Zero. Two. Six.'

The man pushes me. And I stumble forward. And when I look back at him, he is waving me on. Waving me towards the light. The light shining to the dirty warehouse floor.

'Go,' he whispers. 'Stand there.'

I walk slowly towards the light and when I stand under it the microphone makes a horrible squeak sound. And then the man is talking. His voice booming again. From nowhere. From out of the dark.

'A young girl. Eight years old. Speaks two languages. English and French.'

I blink into the darkness and see small red lights. Lots of small red lights. The red lights of cameras. And computers. And phones.

'We'll start the bidding at one-hundred thousand euro,' the microphone booms.

JAVI

Ugly Yellow Jacket looks up and down the street... waiting. Waiting on the police to get here. And I know. I know as I stare at him that he's not a real policeman. He might be an investigator with the PTU. But he is no police officer. If he was, my hands would be in cuffs by now. Broken arm or no broken arm.

Then I look at the two bullies who tried to beat me up. Throwing punches at the back of my head, kicking my legs. None of them look as if they're rich. As if they can't be bought.

So, I sit up more and drop the satchel from my left shoulder, my good shoulder, before opening it and showing them what's inside.

'Listen to me,' I say. 'If you let me go before the sirens come, I will give each of you ten thousand euro.'

Ugly Yellow Jacket doesn't respond. He just huffs through his nose, but the other two men lean in to take a look.

'What you doing with all that money?' the fat one asks.

'That's how much he got paid for kidnapping two children,' Lenny Moon says. 'Don't touch that money. Those notes, that bag, it'll help put this scumbag behind bars for years.'

He leans his bald head towards me. And now I know. I know

I'm not buying my way out of this. This bald idiot with the ugly yellow jacket can't be bought.

'I didn't mean to do it. Honest to God above,' I say. 'I didn't mean to take the children. I just—'

'Where the fuck is Sofie Le Saux?' he says through his teeth, his bald head pressing against my head.

'Sofie?' I say.

I close my eyes and think of her little face. How sweet she was when she accepted a mint from me this morning. How scared she looked tied to the bed.

'Where has she been taken to?'

I laugh. And he kicks my chest and I fall back to the road. Again.

'I'm not laughing at you,' I say staring up at the sky. 'I'm laughing that you think I know where she is.'

When I strain my neck to look up at him, he seems confused. He stares back over his shoulders at the two men standing behind him.

I hold my right shoulder with my left hand while Ugly Yellow Jacket picks my satchel up from my chest. And as I suck a breath in through my teeth, to make the pain go away, I hear it. I hear it in the distance. The siren. Coming this way. Coming to take me to jail until I'm seventy.

'Where has Sofie been taken to? Tell me. Tell me before the police get here!' he says, standing over me, gripping all of my money.

'I'll need to go to a hospital before I go to prison,' I say.

'What the fuck?' he says. He holds his foot against my chest. 'You think your cuts and bruises are our concern right now? With a little girl still missing?' He bends down and slaps at my right elbow, making the pain shoot as high as my jaw. 'Where has she been taken to?' he spits down at me.

'I don't know!' I shout back.

'What do you know?' he asks.

'Nothing,' I say.

'Who did you take her to? At the river?'

'I do not know. Honest to God above,' I say.

'Stop playing games with me, Horata. Tell me. Tell me before the police get here and take you away. If you tell me,' he says, dropping to one knee, 'I'll get you help. I'll let the police know you were cooperative. That you tried to support the investigation. In this kind of case, that will buy five years of freedom.'

'Better add another five years in prison for writing off our cars!' the fat one says from behind Lenny Moon.

'Shhhh!' Lenny says, spinning around. But there's no silence. Not around here. Not anymore. Not with the siren getting louder and louder and nearer and nearer.

'You better hope that's the PTU coming first,' he says. 'Because we're the ones who can help you. We can. If that's the police, you're fucked. They're gonna take you straight to a prison. And with the charges you face, Horata, you're not gonna come out of that prison till it's right about time for you to get prostate cancer. Tell me, tell me before that siren gets here, where did you take her to?'

'You know where I took her to,' I say, gripping my right shoulder. It's so painful. *So* fucking painful. 'I took her to the river. I took her to where Vlatva meets Labe. That's where I was told to take both of them. That's where I got the money.'

Ugly Yellow Jacket stares at the notes inside the satchel he's gripping, then back down at me.

'Who told you to take them to the Vlatva and Labe? Who gave you the instructions?'

'I...I,' I shout as the siren gets louder 'I don't know any names. I don't know anybody.'

'How the fuck did you know to bring them to Vlatva and Labe?'

He tosses the satchel aside, and grabs my collar, shaking me.

'I was told to,' I say.

'By who?' he shouts right into my face. Spitting into my face.

'By phone!' I say. 'By phone.'

He leans closer, his nose pressed to mine as the sirens blast loud.

'I will help you. I will make sure your sentence is reduced, Javi Horata. Just give it to me,' he says. 'Give me that phone number!'

LENNY

18:29

Lenny stands, his two legs astride Horata, his head still swaying, and his mind still whirring as he takes the phone from the man lying on the road beneath him.

It feels to Lenny as if it was months ago he was offered a job with the PTU, not literally a matter of hours. Now here he was, stood wide-legged over a trafficker on a dirt road on the outskirts of Prague, his temples throbbing, his chin stinging, his clothes weighing heavy and damp from his daring dive into the choppy waters of the River Labe.

Despite tracking down the kidnapper, and gaining access to Sophie Le Saux's Kindle, Lenny remains unsure he is fit for purpose as a PI. No investigator he watched on TV ever got themselves into such a dire physical and mental state. In two car crashes. He's been in a river. Lain unconscious on the bed of a forest. And cringing in an innocent man's home while he called out Sofie's name. But what's mostly consuming his spinning mind right now is that while even he can admit he's made progress in this case, an awareness has engulfed him that Sofie Le Saux is further from his reach than she has been at any stage during his investigation.

'That is the number,' Horata says as Lenny takes his phone. 'I was told to bring the children to Vlatva and Labe at four p.m. They tried to screw me on the money. That is all I know. I know no names. But that is the number I rang.'

Lenny glares at Horata's screen while shovelling his other hand into the pocket of his heavy yellow puffer jacket to retrieve his own phone. Then he glances over both shoulders, desperate to locate the source of the siren wailing. But he can't see any flashing blue lights. Not yet.

When he spins back to the phones, he notices the concrete beneath his feet is pulsating again. Swaying. Swirling. Blues and purples. Yet despite the headrush, he begins to stab the phone number displaying on Horata's cheap mobile phone into his own iPhone and is about to hit the final digit — a six — when Horata pipes up.

'Tell the police that I helped. That I was cooperative, yes?'

Lenny doesn't answer. Instead, he blows out a long exhale before sinking to his hunkers, his stomach now spinning in tandem with his head.

'Oh fuck,' he gulps as his cheeks bloat.

He tastes it before it spews from him, slapping against the concrete next to Horata's worn shoes.

'Holy hell, are you okay?' the rotund man asks.

The three strangers look at each other, then back at the bald investigator heaving bile into the ground as the siren pierces and echoes around them.

Suddenly, Lenny's body slumps forward slowly and both phones clatter to the concrete. Then his cheek gently presses to the cold concrete while his puffer jacket slaps against the puddle of bile he just spewed.

The three men look stunned at Lenny's limp body, then up at

the blue light as it flashes, its deafening siren not loud enough to bring Lenny back around.

Horata sits more upright on the road, his breathing huffed, his right arm lying limp across his lap. He stares at Lenny's body laid flat out in front of him, then at the police car as it races towards them, its siren whistling to a high pitch, sudden stop as the wheels skid next to the two damaged vehicles.

The bespectacled man shouts something in Czech at the two uniformed officers as they exit their car, pointing at Horata first, then describing the yellow lump in the road with a shrug of a shoulder.

'PTU?' one police man says his bottom lip sticking out, his head shaking.

While they are talking about him, Lenny's mouth is ajar, his throat gurgling a light snore as he inhales, his mind in a different location entirely. Back home. Back home with Celina. And Jacob and Jared.

One police man steps around his limp body, to grab at Horata, causing him to yelp and cry in pain. Despite his limp, broken arm, his hands are locked in cuffs behind his back before he is dragged towards the police car, wincing, and wailing.

The other uniform speaks in Czech to both innocent men next to Lenny's body, scribbling notes into his miniature pad with a rush. Then he suddenly stops writing, his head pivoting in search of the wheels he just heard—swooshing in the distance. Coming their way

The other officer holds Horata's head down, pushing him into the back of the patrol car as he squints across the bridge, seeing a black BMW appearing out of the mist. Then he slaps the back door closed on Horata's face and looks back at his colleague with his bottom lip sticking out.

When the BMW screeches to a stop at the bridge, a man wearing a black suit to match his shiny black car exits, twisting his cufflinks.

'I'm wif the PTU, I'll take this from 'ere, mate,' he says.

He smoothly pulls an ID badge from the inside pocket of his tight blazer and holds it aloft between the pinch of two fingers.

'The PTU is real?' the rotund man says, nudging the bespectacled man. 'Wake up, Lenny.'

He kicks Lenny's leg, trying but failing to bring the investigator around.

'Your officer here has taken too many blows to the head, I think,' the bespectacled man says to the suit.

The PTU officer hunkers beside Lenny and places two fingers to his neck.

'He'll be alrigh'. I'll take him wif me. I'll also take him,' he says, pointing towards the police car.

'Non, non, non,' one of the uniforms says. 'Javi Horata is coming with us.'

'Nope,' the suit says. 'That's my man. On charges of people trafficking.'

'We have no proof of people trafficking,' the uniform says. 'We only have proof of car theft. We're bringing him to Cenkov Police Station on charges of theft.'

The suit whistles, the tune to a TV show nobody conscious is likely to have ever seen, then he subtly shakes his handsome head.

'Facking cops,' he says, his Cockney accent thick. 'Every facking time.'

He pulls a phone out of his tight trousers pocket, then paces towards his BMW to make a call, his fingers combing through his thick jet-black quiff.

While Lenny remains comatose, his body flat out on a puddle of vomit, his mouth still sucking in the air that is gargling in the back of his throat, the rotund man and the bespectacled man begin to question the police officers about their cars, the conversation heating as they seek answers about their insurance rights.

The PTU officer stuns the argument into a silence when he approaches, his phone call clearly swift.

'Right, listen,' he says, 'It was the PTU who investigated the man you 'ave in your car there. This guy...' He points down at Lenny's bloated yellow jacket. 'Handed him over to you, alrigh'. Let your arrest records show that. If you do, I'll let you take him. But I,' he stabs a finger to the chest of his pristine black suit, 'Am takin' this fella wiv me.' He drops his point to Lenny beneath him before bending down to hug both arms around the bloated yellow jacket.

'Ah, wha' a' fack is this?' he calls out, stepping backwards.

He shakes his hands, spraying bile to the concrete as he spits and cusses.

'That is his own vomit,' the bespectacled man says. 'If you do not mind Mr in the suit. I uh...' The bespectacled man shuffles towards the suit. 'I do not want to take much of your time, but do you...' He refixes the glasses on the bridge of his nose. 'Do you know anything about car insurance? You see, he crashed into my car, but it was he,' he points at Lenny's body, 'who caused it, and I think it might be mostly all his fault.' He spins around to point at the police car Horata is now sat in the back of, wincing more from the fact that he got caught than the pain throbbing up and down his right arm.

The handsome PI officer raises a perfectly plucked eyebrow at the bespectacled man.

'Wha' a' fack are you talkin' about? 'Ere, gimme a hand, mate.'

He bends back down to wrap his arms around Lenny's chest again, then nods towards the feet.

The bespectacled man hesitates at first before eventually wrapping his arms around Lenny's legs, helping the handsome suit to lift the damp, heavy body to the back of the black BMW.

'I would say he can pay my insurance first, and then maybe the guy in the police car can pay everybody's insurance, if he has insurance. That's the other thing. What if no insurance pays out?'

They swing Lenny's limp body into the back seat, then the handsome suit slaps his hands together, nodding at the bespectacled man for helping him.

'Sorry,' he says. 'I don't know wha' a' fack you're talkin' about, mate.'

He walks to the other side of the BMW and sweeps the driver's door open.

'Excuse, excuse, excuse!' the rotund man shouts after him. 'Excuse!'

The rotund man bends down next to the puddle of vomit, then rushes towards the suit.

'Your investigator's phone,' he says.

The suit pinches the iPhone, then climbs inside his BMW and after stabbing a finger to the GO button, making the electric engine purr, he tosses the phone over his shoulder, landing it with a poof on the cushion of Lenny's damp yellow jacket.

SOFIE

I rolled around in the back of the white van for longer this time. Much, much longer. Like a whole afternoon. Or a whole evening. Or a whole whatever time of day it is. It might even be dark when he slides that side door open. Whenever he slides that side door open. The van has been stopped for a long time now. The engine off. The air cold. So, so cold. The only good thing is I don't have to try to stop myself from rolling around the back anymore. When it was driving I had to sit myself into the corner, near the door, holding myself up by pushing one foot to the side of the van and the other to the back door, my head bent towards my legs. I stayed there for most of the drive. Unless he was taking a big corner, and then I would tumble across the dirty metal floor. My hands hurt every time I had to roll onto my back. But for most of the drive I just sat in the corner, bent forward, trying to hold on with my feet. Thinking about what happened back at the warehouse.

I begin to think about lots of red lights. So, so many red lights. Maybe a hundred of them. Or a thousand. I don't know. Nobody could count that many that fast. Because I was only there for less than a minute. I couldn't really understand what the microphone was saying. Not until he repeated the same number over and over again while I was staring out at those red lights.

'One hundred and sixty thousand. That's one hundred and sixty thousand. Once at one-hundred and sixty thousand.... Twice...' A horrible noise came from the microphone. And then the light over my head switched off and the man with the big round nose ran on to the stage and grabbed me by my arm again.

'Fantastic,' he said. 'You did fantastic.'

He dragged me down the steps, past some children with some adults in the warehouse, then through the big doors that we walked in earlier, and back out to the car park. The cold car park. He told me to shut up as he dragged me, without me even saying anything, then he slid open the side door of his horrible dirty van again and pushed me inside.

Then we drove. And we drove. And we drove. For so long. So, so long. So long I don't know how long. Hours. Maybe four hours. Or eight. With me trying to not roll around in the back by holding one foot to the side wall and the other to the door, my head hanging lower and lower.

While my head was getting lower and lower, I was getting angrier and angrier. And it made me feel that trying to kick him when he was carrying me on his shoulders earlier wasn't enough. I should have kicked his face. Kicked his eyes. That's what I should do. Kick his eyes when he slides open the side door of the van again. Kick him in the eyes so that he can't see. And then I can run off, even with my hands tied behind my back I'll still get away from him if he can't see.

'That's what you get for stealing my Kindle!' I could shout at him. Then I'd run. I'd run and I'd run, and I'd run as far away as I can.

But now that the van has stopped I am thinking I'm not going to do that. It's too scary. I might try to kick him in the eyes and then he'd be too strong for me. He'd lean on top of me and squish me into the back of the van. Then he might try to do what I did. He might try to make me go blind for trying to make him go blind.

I hear a noise. And I sit up straighter. Far away at first. A choo-choo. And I know. Even though it's far away. That it's a train.

I stand up in the back of the van and lean to the side door, listening as the choo-choo gets louder and louder. It doesn't stop. It shoots straight by our van. So really loud. So, so loud. Until the choo-choo sound gets further and further away... until its gone. And then I sit back down, back into the corner I sat in for hours. My stomach talks again while I am bent over my legs. Telling me she is hungry.

That's when I hear the front door of the van opening, and then slapping shut. Footsteps.... And now I know that I am definitely not going to kick him in the eyes when he opens that side door. I'll just do what he says. Then I'll think of another plan. Another way I can try to get out of here.

There's a crunch sound at the side door before it slides open. When I look around, I can barely see him in the dark. And he can barely see me. Because he leans forward to look up and down the van until I crawl out of the corner towards him. I try to look over his shoulder, for any clues. Any clues at all. But it's too dark. Too dark to see anything but the different colours of black in the sky.

He lifts me up to his shoulder again, my stomach bent over him, then he walks me across a wet path, his big boots splashing in the puddles. The puddles are the only noise I can hear, apart from my belly talking. And it's the only thing I can see. Until he spins me, and tumbles me forward, and I land on my feet in a small puddle, staring up at him.

'Can I have my Kindle? Please?' I ask.

'Shut up,' he says.

I look around us at all of the dark. At nothing. Just the different colour blacks... until a shadow walks towards me. A big shadow. The shadow of a big, big man. As big a man as I have ever seen. Tall. And fat. And wide.

When he gets close, he gasps, then drops one knee into a puddle and grabs me by both shoulders. That's when I see his face. His big red face. His white hair and his white beard. He looks like Father Christmas. The Father Christmas who always forgot me.

'Money!' the man with the big, round nose says.

The man with the rosy cheeks and white beard drops a bag from his shoulder and Big Nose opens it and looks inside.

He doesn't say anything. He doesn't say 'bye'. He just zips the bag back up and spins away and walks back to his van, sliding the side door closed and then getting back into the driver's seat with his bag of money.

I want to shout after him. I want to know where my Kindle is. But the big man with the rosy cheeks and white beard is staring at me. Scaring me. Scaring me to keep quiet.

'Ma nam iz Viktor,' he says, holding a hand to my cheek.

I stare down at the wet path instead of staring at Viktor. Instead of staring at his rosy cheeks. Then I hear it. In the distance. The choo-choo sound again. And I know... I already know...

'Vot iz your nam?' he says.

I close my eyes, my head still staring down, as the choo-choo gets louder and louder and my body shakes and shivers. From the cold. And from the fright.

'Sofie,' I say, tears falling out of my eyes. 'My name is Sofie Le Saux.'

I sniff up my nose and when I open my eyes and look up, he puts his thumb to my face to wipe the tears away. Then, he grabs me under the arms. And lifts me. Now I am bent over his shoulder. Bent over his shoulder as he runs, my tummy bouncing up and down against him as the noise of the train rattles and shakes, zooming towards us. It's so loud when it reaches us. So, so loud. Then I feel him climbing, lifting me higher. And I fall. Landing on my face. On a wooden floor. A wooden floor that is moving. Shaking and rocking and rattling and moving. Speeding.

LENNY

19:00

The wheels smoothly swishing across the maze of rural roads never purred loudly enough to wake Lenny from his deep sleep, but the screech of the brakes as they squeak to a sudden stop on the edge of the city of Prague finally do.

He rolls over in the backseat with a grunt and a huff, and as his eyes begin to blink back to life he finds himself staring at black sheepskin mat, his brain filling with blood, his eyes bulging and red.

He hears an indicator tick, then swallows with a heavy gulp, before twisting himself up to a sitting position, leaving him staring through the gap of the two seats in front.

When he inches forward to take the driver's profile in, he notices the red light they have stopped at, so he sits back, his mind whirring and flashing with each tick of the indicator.

'Where you taking me?' he asks the thick head of black hair.

The driver stretches the arm of his tight-fitted suit before extending his index finger, causing Lenny to squint out the side window at the sign on the opposite side of the street.

'To a hospital? No, no, no. I'm fine. I feel fine. I just...' Lenny grips his head with both hands, shoving the balls of his palms into his eye sockets and twisting them back and forth.

'You've got severe concussion, mate. Story goes you've been in two car crashes and went for a swim in the River Labe. Look atcha face, mate.'

Lenny lets the grip of his crown go, so he can lean forward to soak in the rear-view mirror. His eyes look heavy and aged. And his stubbled chin is matted with dry blood.

'Shit,' he whispers as memories flood his throbbing head.

The car pulls off, and the indicator finally stops, offering a sliver of respite to the pulsing in his temples. He feels down his jacket. Noticing the rolls of puff have all sunken to the bottom.

'In a river?'

The driver doesn't respond, too busy reversing the BMW into a narrow bay on the front row of the hospital's car park. When the car beeps to a stop, he finally turns his handsome face to his pale passenger.

'Check yourself in, mate. Tell 'em you've suffered a concussion.'

Lenny holds his eyes closed before pivoting his head to glare out at the double-door entrance to the hospital.

'Why did I jump in a river?' he asks.

The driver smirks, causing a deep dimple to sink on one of his cheeks.

'After some guy,' he says.

'A guy?'

'A trafficker.'

Lenny's beady eyes blink rapidly again, then he tilts his chin ever so slightly. Remembering.

'Javi Horata.'

'That's 'im.'

'I need to find him. I have to find him...'

'You did, mate. The brass have taken him into custody. But you took him down. The PTU took him down, mate.'

Lenny's mouth pops open.

'The girl. The blonde girl. French.'

'Sofie.'

'Yes!' he says. 'Where is she?'

The driver shrugs, then spins around in his seat again, gripping the steering wheel.

'I gotta go, mate. So... if you just tell a nurse you've suffered concussion, you'll be looked after in there.'

The handsome suit nods towards the hospital entrance again, then stretches his finger to the GO button, causing the electric engine to purr.

After blowing out his cheeks, exhausted, Lenny snatches the back door open and steps into the cold. When he's about to slam the door closed, he notices his iPhone lying face down on the back seat, so he reaches across to swipe it up, then shovels it into the pocket of his damp yellow jacket before offering a muted 'thank you' to the handsome driver.

As soon as he slams the door closed, the BMW wooshes off and Lenny can shuffle his way across the zebra crossing that will lead him to the glassed entrance of the recently-built hospital lobby. He shivers as he walks, his head still spinning and swaying.

When he enters the echoey reception area he stares around at the patients waiting impatiently, some with obvious injuries, most with mystery illnesses, then stands for his turn to talk with one of the two ladies dressed in maroon scrubs currently working the front desk.

He recalls his conversation with Celina earlier as he stares at the back of the head of the person in front of him. He often starts his thought processes by thinking about her pretty face. Celina told him Jared and Jacob were happy in the back garden. She showed him Jacob and Jared happy in the back garden. Everybody's happy. Except him. Stood in line at a strange Emergency Room in a strange hospital on the outskirts of a strange city, his head throbbing, his chin stinging, his clothes glued to his shrivelling, pale skin.

He recalls why he isn't at home with them. With Celina and his boys. He's in Prague on a job. A job to find a missing girl. Sofie Le Saux. A young girl who could be who-knows-where by now.

'Dalsi!' a women's voice calls out. 'Dalsi!' Louder this time.

Lenny is nudged by the woman standing behind him, then offers a shrug of an apology before stepping towards the desk.

'English?' he asks, his eyes squinting.

'Yes, sir,' the woman replies, looking Lenny up and down. 'How can we help you?'

'I uh...' Lenny shakes his head. 'I've been in a car crash. Two car crashes. I believe. I'm uh...'

'You're concussed, sir,' the woman says, rushing out from behind her desk.

'I am, yeah. How did you... how did you know?' Lenny asks before the woman wraps one arm around him, then leads him towards a door at the back of the reception desk.

'I can tell by your eyes, sir,' she says.

She kicks the door open with the sole of her boot, Lenny's weight leaning heavy against her. Then she helps him navigate a turn in the corridor before she scoots a curtain aside with her free hand and heaves his wiry frame to the edge of a gurney.

'Sir, if you just sit, I'll get a nurse to come see you. Soon as one is available.'

Lenny nods, then blinks at the woman who helped him to the emergency unit before he sweeps his legs to the side, attempting to lie down, offering a grunt and a huff to nobody. When he rests his head to the gurney and closes his eyes, he hears the rush around him, the beeping of distant machines, the clapping of shoes off the hard floors, somebody sniffling a cry in the distance. Then he sees her face again. Smiling at him from a one-sheet.

Sofie Le Saux. She was taken on a speedboat. That's why he jumped into a river. He was chasing after Sofie. His lips crease into a tight smile as recalls Liam McLyn. Tracked down. Found. Probably still hugging Olette Lee somewhere safe in the city. Olette Lee. He recalls her marble eyes. And then the time her long fingernail touched high on his thigh while she was driving. His lips crease even more, and to eradicate the guilt, he blows out his cheeks, then pushes himself to a sitting position on the gurney, so he can wrestle the phone from his jacket pocket.

He stabs a finger at the screen to find he was just about to call somebody when his phone was last turned off. Not call somebody. He was about to store a number into the phone. That's right! The number Javi Horata had given to him at the scene of the car smash. The number of the contact Horata was using to sell the children on.

He counts the digits he has already punched in and realises he is only one short from completing a whole phone number.

'I remember,' he says, puffing a relief-laugh through both nostrils and standing from the gurney. 'I remember!'

His pointed leather shoes squeak against the hard floor as he excitedly thumbs the number six, completing a whole phone number. Then he stabs at the green CALL Button and presses the phone tight to his ear.

'Lenny Moon,' she says, her tone familiar. Too fucking familiar.

Lenny takes the phone from his ear and stares at the screen, stunned to see her name displayed across the top.

'Olette?' he says, his brow dipping, his bottom lip popping open. 'You? Javi Horata was selling Liam and Sofie to you?'

To be continued....

WHATEVER HAPPENED TO OLETTE LEE?

Book SIX
in ***The Lenny Moon Series***.

Check out the opening chapter on the next page.

OLETTE

The top tips of the yellow grass sway more rapidly as the breeze whips, whistling up and then across the river diagonally. Liam shakes in my arms before gripping me tighter, squeezing both elbows into my waist while we wait on the sirens to reach us.

It's strange to be here right now. Hugging a boy who was swiped off the streets of Prague this morning. But I am mostly struck numb that the jittery, sweaty hopeful who arrived for his interview in a yellow puff jacket traced two trafficked children down within a matter of hours.

'I can see them,' Liam says, loosening his grip.

He points towards the horizon at the blue lights flashing in tandem with the sirens. And as we both watch, I lean my chin onto the top of his hair.

'You will be in your mother and father's arms in thirty-minutes,' I whisper.

My pocket suddenly vibrates, and I take my phone out, staring at the number that belongs to the jittery, sweaty hopeful from this morning. The hopeful so dumb he dived into a river. The hopeful so intelligent he traced two children on his first day.

'Hello,' I say, answering.

I hold the phone tight to my ear, while I shiver with the cold.

'Olette?' he says. And I can tell already by the way he said my name that he knows. He *definitely* knows. And suddenly I stop shivering. 'You? Javi Horata was selling Liam and Sofie to you?'

The sirens whistle to a piercing stop as I press the phone tighter to my ear, my lips snapped tight together, saying nothing. Because there's nothing to say. Not yet.

I kiss the top of Liam's head before taking the phone from my ear and stabbing my thumb against the red button, ending the call. Ending the inquisition that would inevitably erupt should I even attempt to explain myself to Lenny Moon.

'Fuck,' I shout over Liam's head towards Erik as he exits the first BMW. 'I've been compromised!'

'Olette?' Liam says, his voice pure and innocent as his face turns to look up at me, in shock. In the twenty minutes I stood hugging him on this speedboat I held the same delicate tone; caring, maternal. He didn't experience me any other way. Not until I shouted a swear word over his head in the direction of one of our investigators. But I don't have time to explain myself to Liam, not when I've just been compromised. So I kiss the top of his head again, then I leap over the side of the boat and run. I run as fast as I can.

'Who's in the second car?' I shout at Erik as we run towards each other.

'Julien,' Erik shouts.

'Okay, well, I'm taking your car. You and Julien can escort the boy back to The Grand Hotel, yes? The boy is on that boat.'

'Yes ma'am!' he shouts as he races by me. Full speed.

As I continue running towards the first BMW, Julien exits the second car, swiping his Ray-Bans from his face like only he can swipe Ray-Bans from a face.

'You okay, Olette?'

'No,' I shout over the car. 'The boy's on the boat. Get him into his parent's hands as quickly as you can!'

I pull the door of the BMW open and hop inside, stabbing my long fingernail against the GO button.

'I don't fucking believe this!' I say as I slam the door closed, my foot already pressed against the gas pedal.

When Lenny Moon first entered my office at the top of Empire Tower this morning I felt he was the kind of man who couldn't play Cluedo without getting lost. Let alone an effective private investigator. Yet half a day later not only has he tracked down two swiped children, but he's compromised me. Compromised himself. Compromised the entire People Trafficking Unit.

'Siri,' I direct the dashboard, before a blue light appears on the screen, rotating. 'Take me to Clyss Airport.'

The light spins and spins while I drum my fingers against the steering wheel.

'Clyss Airport,' the robotic voice tells me. 'Estimated arrival time seven, thirty-three p.m.

A map appears on the dashboard and as it does, my phone buzzes on the passenger seat again, his name flashing at me.

'Fuck you, Moon,' I spit at the phone. Through gritted teeth. 'Fuck you, you meddling fuck.'

When the vibrating stops, and the BMW picks up speed, I shout at the screen on the dashboard again.

'Siri, call Hilda.'

The circle rotates, and rotates, until a ring tone plays through the speakers.

'Miss Lee,' she says, answering.

'Hilda,' I say. 'Organise a flight for me from Clyss Airport.'

'Vot is wrong, Miss Lee?' she says, her German accent broad.

'I've been compromised. When Dr Volgt arrives back in the office, tell him. Tell him I've been compromised.'

'How?' Hilda asks.

I sigh, slapping a hand against the steering wheel.

'One of the new recruits. From this morning.'

'Vhich von?' she asks.

'Moon,' I tell her. 'Lenny Moon.'

I hear her typing at her keyboard, calling up his file.

'The bald guy?' she says. 'Irish?'

'That's him.'

I stare at my white knuckles gripping the steering wheel. Tight. Tight and tense.

'How?' she asks.

'He learned I was trying to make a trade.'

'And you need a flight to take you to vhere, Miss Lee...'

'You've just called up his file, Hilda, yes?' I ask.

'I have, Miss Lee,' she says.

'Good,' I say. 'Read it to me.'

'Leonard Joseph Moon. Forty-eight-year-old male. From Dublin, Ireland. But currently lives in Belgium. In a small town called Lier. He is a vidower. His vife died in 2020. He has two children. Twin boys. Names are Jacob and Jared.'

I nod as I recall those notes from the many notes of the many interviewees I sped-read about ahead of their interviews this morning.

'Okay, tell me, where are the twin boys now? With him in Belgium? Or back home in Ireland?

'Looks like they moved to Belgium vith him,' she says. 'To stay at a cottage in Lier belonging to a thirty-eight-year-old female. Miss Celina Pieters.'

'Lier?' I ask.

'Yes. Lier. It is a small town on the outskirts of Antwerp.'

'Right. Okay,' I say. 'Well, I guess that's where I need to go to. Organise for me to land as close to Lier as I possibly can, Hilda.'

'Yes, Miss Lee,' she says. 'I'm on it, Miss Lee.'

FROM INTERNATIONAL BESTSELLING AUTHOR

DAVID B. LYONS

WHATEVER HAPPENED TO OLETTE LEE?

BOOK SIX OF THE LENNY MOON NOVELLA SERIES

WHATEVER HAPPENED TO OLETTE LEE?

ACKNOWLEDGMENTS

This entire series is dedicated to my devoted readers.

Thank you so much for investing your time and money on my stories. I am really looking forward to your reactions to the final book in this series — Whatever Happened to Olette Lee?

If you have a spare minute, could you please leave a review online for any of the novellas you have read wherever it is you purchased the book from? It would mean a lot.

A big thank you goes to Nastasia and the team at Stardust Books for the wonderful artwork they produce for the covers of these novellas. As well as to my editorial team of Maureen Vincent-Northam, Brigit Taylor, and Deborah Longman.

Made in the USA
Middletown, DE
31 May 2024

55100919R00071